Mary Proctor

Stories of Starland

Mary Proctor

Stories of Starland

ISBN/EAN: 9783337407872

Printed in Europe, USA, Canada, Australia, Japan

Cover: Foto ©Andreas Hilbeck / pixelio.de

More available books at **www.hansebooks.com**

STORIES OF STARLAND

BY

MARY PROCTOR

(Daughter of late Richard A. Proctor)

———

NEW YORK

POTTER & PUTNAM COMPANY

LONDON

G. W. BACON & CO., LIMITED

DEDICATED

TO THE MEMORY OF MY BROTHER

HARRY.

The heavens declare the glory of God; and the firmament sheweth his handiwork.—Psalms.

PREFACE.

THIS book has been a labor of love from the beginning to the end, and I have thoroughly enjoyed conversing with my little friends Harry and Nellie. Now that the book is finished, I leave it with regret.

It is impossible to give all the authorities for my legends of the stars. Many were told to me by my father when I was a little girl, or I found them among books in his library, which is now scattered far and wide. Others are from Grecian mythology, Japanese folk-lore, Hindoo legends, while some of the American Indian stories were found in musty volumes of the Bureau of Ethnology at the Smithsonian Institution.

As for the descriptive astronomy, among my authorities are Professor C. A. Young, Professor Barnard, Agnes M. Clerke, Professor R. S. Ball, Schiaparelli, Flammarion, Professor Todd, Mr. Lowell of Flagstaff, Ariz., and my father, the late Richard A. Proctor.

With the kind permission of Houghton, Mifflin & Co. I have been allowed to use the following selections: "Why the Stars Twinkle," by Oliver Wendell Holmes;

"The Evening Star," by Longfellow; "Lady Moon," by Lord Houghton; and "The New Moon," by Mrs. Follen. The editor of *St. Nicholas* has kindly given me permission to include the poems "The Four Sunbeams," by M. K. B.; "Estelle's Astronomy," by Delia Hart Stone; and "Seven Little Indian Stars," by Mrs. S. M. B. Piatt. I am indebted to the editor of *Child-Study Monthly* for the little poem "Is It True?" by Morgan Growth. The poem on "The Solar System" is taken from the *Youth's Companion*, with the kind permission of the editor. The verses about "Wynken, Blynken, and Nod" are so familiar to every child that my book of STORIES OF STARLAND would seem incomplete without this poem by Eugene Field. The illustration of a Part of the Milky Way is from a photograph taken by Professor Barnard at the Lick Observatory. Mr. Percival Lowell has also very kindly allowed me to make use of his excellent illustration of the Canals of Mars, taken from Todd's "New Astronomy," published by the American Book Company.

I now submit this little book to my young readers, sincerely hoping its pages may inspire them with a renewed interest in the wonders of Starland.

MARY PROCTOR.

NEW YORK CITY, June, 1898.

CONTENTS.

9

"HARRY."

STORIES OF STARLAND.

LIGHT.

Night has a thousand eyes,
  And the day but one ;
Yet the light of the bright world dies
  With the dying sun.

The mind has a thousand eyes,
  And the heart but one ;
Yet the light of the whole life dies
  When love is done.
              —F. W. BOURDILLON.

THE STORY OF GIANT SUN.

"SISTER, come here and talk to me. I am so tired of being alone."

His sister Mary at once closed her book, and took a chair beside Harry's couch. Poor little Harry was not like other boys. He could not play and run about as they did, for he was a cripple. All the long weary days he had to lie on a couch which was placed under the shady trees during the warm summer season. He had

learned to love the flowers and trees, and the
bright blue sky overhead, and his sister often told
him pretty stories about them. She was just
thinking of telling him one now, when he said
gently :

ANCIENT STORIES OF THE SUN.

" Sister, you have told me so many stories of
the flowers. I wish you would tell me something
about the sky. I have been looking at it for
such a long time, watching the little white clouds
floating across it like boats with silver sails ; and
then I tried to look at the bright yellow sun, but
it dazzles my eyes. Won't you tell me about it,
and where it goes in the evening when we cannot
see it any more ? Is it always ready in the
morning to give us light ? Is it ever late, do you
think ? What would we do if it forgot to come
round the edge of the earth and give us light ? "
he continued anxiously.

" There is no fear of that," said his sister Mary,
laughing at the idea. " But a long time ago
people asked the very same question. In those

days they thought the earth was flat, and surrounded by an ocean without end. The Hindoos supposed that the earth rested upon four elephants, and the four elephants stood on the back of an immense tortoise, which itself floated on the

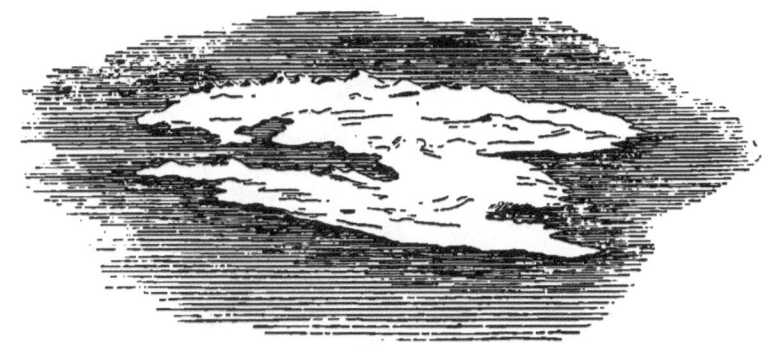

EARTH SUPPOSED TO BE FLAT.

surface of an endless ocean. It was thought that the sun plunged into the ocean when it disappeared in the evening, and some people said they heard a hissing noise when the red-hot body went under the waves.

"But if the sun dropped into the water each evening, how did it happen that next morning it was seen again, as hot and bright as ever? The people could not tell why, so they said that during the night the gods made a new sun to be used the next day."

"That must have kept them busy," said Harry, laughing.

"The good people made up another story about the sun, so that the same one could be

ANCIENT IDEA OF THE EARTH.

saved each night. Just as it was dropping into the ocean, a god named Vulcan, who had a great boat ready, caught it, and all night long he paddled with the blazing sun. Next morning he was ready at sunrise to send the sun up into the sky in the east. He threw it with

so much force that it would go very high, and
when it came down on the other side in the
west, he stood ready to catch it again."

"But where does the sun really go to at
night?" asked Harry curiously. "I should like
to know."

HEAT OF THE SUN.

"We live on a big round globe called Earth,"
replied his sister, "and we travel round the sun,
which gives the earth light and heat. The sun is

ILLUSTRATING DAY AND NIGHT.

like a great lamp in the sky, and when you face
the lamp you see the light, but if you turn away
from it you are in darkness. As the earth goes
around the sun, it whirls around like a huge top;

first one side and then the other is turned to the
sun and gets sunlight, and so we have day and
night.   If the sun, or the lamp in the sky, went
out and stopped shining, all the light would go
out on the earth, and we would
miss its heat as well.

"It is so hot that if it kept
coming nearer and nearer until it
was as far from the earth as the
pretty bright moon, the earth would
get warmer and warmer and melt like a ball of
wax."

"Just like Nellie's doll, then," said Harry,
"when she left it on the grass the other day.
The sun was so hot that day that when Nellie
picked up her doll, she found that its wax face
had melted and the eyes had fallen in.   So the
sun did that," continued Harry, laughing heartily.
"Poor Nellie!   I must tell her that the next time
I see her."

"I can show you something else to prove how
hot the sun is," said Mary, as she picked up a leaf
from the ground.   "Just wait a moment while

I go into the house and get a magnifying-glass."

In a few minutes she returned, holding the glass in one hand and the leaf in the other. She held it so that the sun shone directly upon the glass and passed through it onto the leaf. In a few seconds the leaf began to smoke, and then burn, until a little hole could be seen.

Harry was so surprised that he had to try it for himself, and he looked forward with much delight to a visit from his cousin Nellie.

" Won't I have a lot to tell her?" he said to his sister : " all about the sun's melting her dollie, and how to make the sun burn a hole through a leaf. But the sun cannot be very far away, can it?" he asked.

DISTANCE OF THE SUN.

"Yes, it is very far away," replied Mary. " If a railroad could be made from the earth to the sun, and a train started going at the rate of a mile a minute, it would take days and weeks and years to get there.

"Let me see," said Mary, making a little note in her note-book. "There are sixty minutes in an hour, and twenty-four hours in a day, and three hundred and sixty-five days in a year. Why, Harry, do you know it would take that train nearly one hundred and seventy-five years to get there?"

"It must be very far away, then," said Harry, "more than a hundred miles."

"It is more than a million miles," said Mary. "It is nearly ninety-three millions of miles away. Now let us suppose you want to go to the sun. You would call at the railroad office and ask for a ticket to Sunland. The officer in charge would appear a little surprised, because that is quite a long trip. Then he would look up the cost of the journey in his book, and hand you a mileage book, saying: 'Sir, if you want to save money on this trip, you had better take a mileage book with you, costing two cents for every mile. Even then your fare will be nearly two million dollars.'"

"Then I would say: 'Dear sir, I cannot go, as

I know my sister could not spare all that money. I think I would rather walk to the sun.' How long would it take me to walk there, supposing I could walk?" asked Harry thoughtfully.

"Dear, you would have to keep walking a very long time before you would ever get there. Supposing you walked four miles an hour, and ten hours a day, and kept this up for hundreds of years, you would be more than six thousand years on the way. When you reached the sun you would be footsore and weary, and as old as the hills."

Harry laughed heartily at the idea, and thought again of poor Nellie's doll and the melting wax running like tears down its cheeks.

"But suppose," he asked, his eyes bright with excitement, "someone fired a big cannon at the sun. Would the cannon-ball ever get there?"

Again Mary brought out her little note-book, and, with rather a look of surprise, she said: "Supposing the cannon-ball went as fast as it could go, it would take nine years to reach the sun, and the sound of the explosion would reach there in fourteen years. The cannon-ball would come along first, and five years afterward, if you were living on the sun, you would hear the sound made when the cannon was fired off.

"It takes time for me to walk from the garden to the house, so it takes time for sound to travel from the earth to the sky; and sound travels only one-fifth of a mile in a second. Do you remember the thunderstorm the other day, Harry, that frightened you so?"

"I shall never forget it," said Harry, trembling at the thought. You said, 'Count slowly'; and I counted one, two, three, four, five, up to fifteen."

"Then I said: 'Don't be afraid, brother; the storm is three miles away.'"

"Yes, I remember," said Harry; "and I thought you were very clever, and wondered how you knew."

"It was not so wonderful, after all, was it?" said Mary, laughing.

"Now tell me, sister," said Harry. "Supposing I had a very long arm, and stretched it out toward the sun, and touched it with the tip of my little finger. What would happen?"

"You would never know that you had burned it, for the pain of burning would be one hundred and fifty years going along your little finger, and down your giant arm nearly ninety-three millions of miles long, before it at last reached your brain. Then it would let you know that one hundred and fifty years before you had burned your little finger."

Harry stretched out his little arm in the direction of the sun, and, looking at it critically, laughed at the idea of a giant arm millions of miles long.

"It is too short by several inches," said his sister, reading his thoughts, and joining in the laugh. "It would take hundreds and hundreds of little arms as long as yours, would it not? Now what else do you want to know about the sun?"

SIZE OF THE SUN.

" If you are not very tired, sister," said Harry coaxingly, " I should like to know how large it is. Is it as large as the earth ? "

" Ever so much larger," replied Mary. " It is

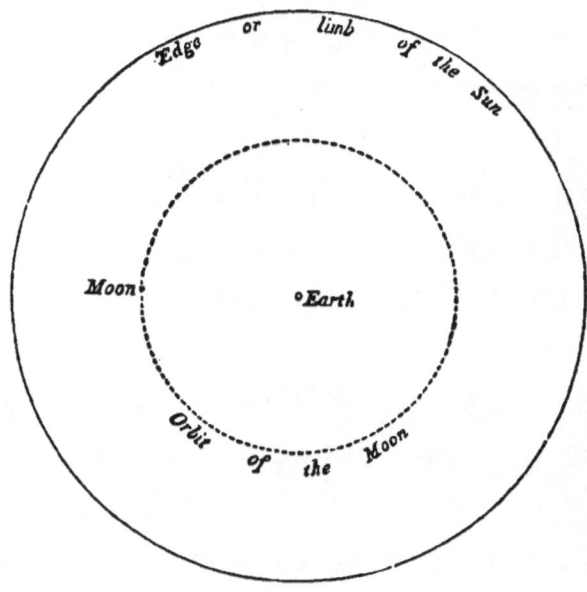

so large that if it were cut up into a million parts, each part would be larger than the earth. If we could weigh the sun in a pair of giant scales, it would take over three hundred thousand globes as heavy as the earth to make the scales even. If the sun were hollowed out, and the earth placed in the center, there would be room for the moon as well. Now the moon is thousands of miles from the earth, and yet the edge of the sun would be thousands of miles from the moon, as you will see in the picture. If a tunnel could be made through the center of the sun, and a train started going at the rate of a mile a minute, it would take six hundred days for the train to reach the other side of the tunnel. If this same train went around the edge of the sun it would take five years. A train going around the earth would take seventeen days to complete the journey."

"But suppose we went around the sun in a big steamer, like the one Uncle Robert came over in; how long would that take?" asked Harry curiously.

"Only fifteen years," said his sister, laughing. "If you had started when you were a little baby you would still have five more years to travel before you would get back again to the starting-point."

" Then the sun must be very large." said Harry
thoughtfully. " Let us call it GIANT SUN.
Has it always been as large as it is now ? "

THE SUN IN THE DAYS OF ITS YOUTH.

" Ever so much larger," replied Mary.

" Once upon a time it was a ball of glowing
gas reaching as far as the path of the last planet.

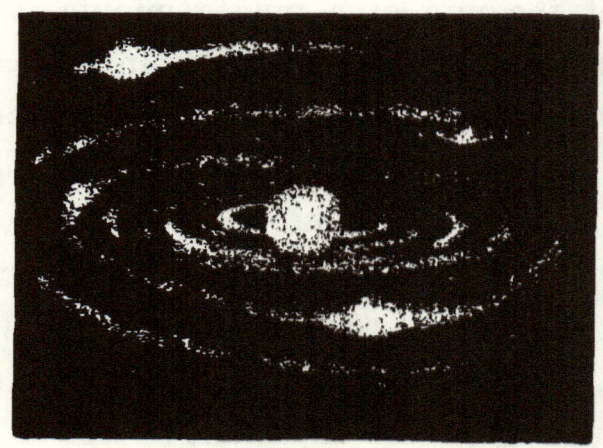

THE SUN AND PLANETS FORMING OUT OF STAR-MIST.

The ball whirled around rapidly and the outer
edge cooled. A ring formed and separated from
the ball and whirled around on its own account,
until it broke up into fragments. One of the
fragments drew all the others toward it, and

another ball was formed, but quite a small ball
this time, called a planet. Just like the central
ball, the planet kept whirling around, threw off
a ring, the ring broke up into little pieces, and
the pieces, coming together, made a little moon.
The planet is Neptune, and it still has only one
moon. Meanwhile the ball in the center kept
whirling around, other rings formed other planets
with their attendant moons, completing the family
of Giant Sun.

"The Sun is in the center and his planets circle
around him. Next to him is playful little
Mercury, then beautiful Venus, then our own
planet Earth. Beyond it, we find ruddy Mars,
the four hundred and fifty baby planets, giant
planet Jupiter, the ringed planet Saturn, and
the last two planets, Uranus and Neptune. All
these planets are under the control of the sun,
and cannot get away from him."

"What is the sun made of?" asked Harry.

"Of iron and copper and silver, and many
other things we can find on earth; but the sun is
so hot that they are melted together into a mass

like glue. This is the center of the sun. Outside is a shell of bright clouds, from which rosy
flames leap to a height of thousands of miles
above the surface of the sun. All around the
edge of the sun, and reaching millions of miles
beyond it, is the pearly light of the corona like
a crown of glory. The pearly corona fades away
into a soft beam of light."

"How beautiful the sun must be!" said Harry,
as he listened attentively to his sister. "But is it
all alone in the sky, and does it not have any
little stars to play with?"

"It is not at all lonely," said Mary, laughing
at the idea of the stars as playthings for Giant
Sun, "and is kept quite busy looking after its
large family of planets. I will tell you about
them to-morrow, or nurse will scold me for tiring
you. And now, good-by, my dear. Don't forget
all I have told you about Giant Sun."

"Forget! how could I, sister? It is better
than any fairy tale I have ever heard. Giant
Sun! Why you have told me enough to keep me
thinking all day and all night. Here comes Nellie.

Hello! Nellie, come here and let me tell you all about GIANT SUN, and how he melted your dollie for you the other day."

"Melted my dollie!" said a pretty little golden-haired girl, as she tripped like a little fairy up the garden-path. "So he melted my dollie, did he? I should like to see him do it again!" Tears came into her eyes at the thought of her sad experience. Since then, however, a china head had replaced the melted wax, and Nellie's fickle little heart had been comforted. So the tears soon vanished in a smile as she showed her new treasure to Harry.

ON THE SETTING SUN.

Those evening clouds, that setting ray,
And beauteous tint, serve to display
   Their great Creator's praise ;
Then let the short-lived thing called man,
Whose life's comprised within a span,
   To Him his homage raise.

We often praise the evening clouds,
  And tints so gay and bold,
But seldom think upon our God,
  Who tinged these clouds with gold.
            —Sir Walter Scott.

SUN.

GIANT SUN AND LITTLE EARTH.

THE FOUR SUNBEAMS.

BY M. K. B.

Four little sunbeams came earthward one day,
Shining and dancing along on their way,
   Resolved that their course should be blest.
" Let us try," they all whispered, " some kindness to do,
Not seek our own pleasuring all the day through,
   Then meet in the eve at the west."

One sunbeam ran in at a low cottage door,
And played " hide-and-seek " with a child on the floor,
   Till baby laughed loud in his glee,
And chased with delight his strange playmate so bright,
The little hands grasping in vain for the light
   That ever before them would flee.

One crept to the couch where an invalid lay,
And brought him a dream of the sweet summer day,
   Its bird-song and beauty and bloom ;
Till pain was forgotten and weary unrest,
And in fancy he roamed through the scenes he loved best,
   Far away from the dim, darkened room.

One stole to the heart of a flower that was sad,
And loved and caressed her until she was glad,
   And lifted her white face again ;
For love brings content to the lowliest lot,
And finds something sweet in the dreariest spot,
   And lightens all labor and pain.

And one, where a little blind girl sat alone,
Not sharing the mirth of her playfellows, shone
  On hands that were folded and pale,
And kissed the poor eyes that had never known sight,
That never would gaze on the beautiful light
  Till angels had lifted the veil.

At last, when the shadows of evening were falling,
And the sun, their great father, his children was calling,
  Four sunbeams sped into the west.
All said: " We have found that in seeking the pleasure
Of others, we fill to the full our own measure,"
  Then softly they sank to their rest.
                    —*St. Nicholas*, December, 1879.

THE SUN.

Somewhere it is always light;
  For when 'tis morning here,
In some far distant land 'tis night,
  And the bright moon shines there.

When you've retired and gone to sleep,
  They are just rising there;
And morning o'er the hill doth creep
  When it is evening here.

And other distant lands there be
  Where it is always night;
For weeks the sun they never see,
  The stars alone give light.

But though 'tis dark both night or day
   It is as wondrous quite
That when the night has passed away,
   The sun for weeks gives light.

Yes, while you sleep the sun shines bright,
   The sky is blue and clear ;
For weeks and weeks there is no night
   But always daylight there.

THE FAMILY OF GIANT SUN.

THE next morning, when Mary came out in the garden to sit with Harry, she was surprised to see an audience of three instead of one: Harry, whose face beamed with delight when he saw her; Nellie, who was seated in a tiny rocking chair beside him, and Nellie's doll.

"You see, dollie wants to know all about Giant Sun, too," Nellie gravely informed Mary. "I never could remember all, and she might remember what I forget. Besides, she must learn some day. That is what mamma said about me. I heard her," Nellie continued wisely, as she looked up at Mary. "Do you mind telling me about the sky-people too?"

"Mind? Why you little bit of a doll baby," laughed Mary, as she picked her up, doll and all, and hugged her, "if you and dollie promise not to go to sleep, you can stay here as long as you want to. But does Aunt Agnes know you are here, Nellie; or have you run away from home?"

"No, I have not run away," said Nellie earn-

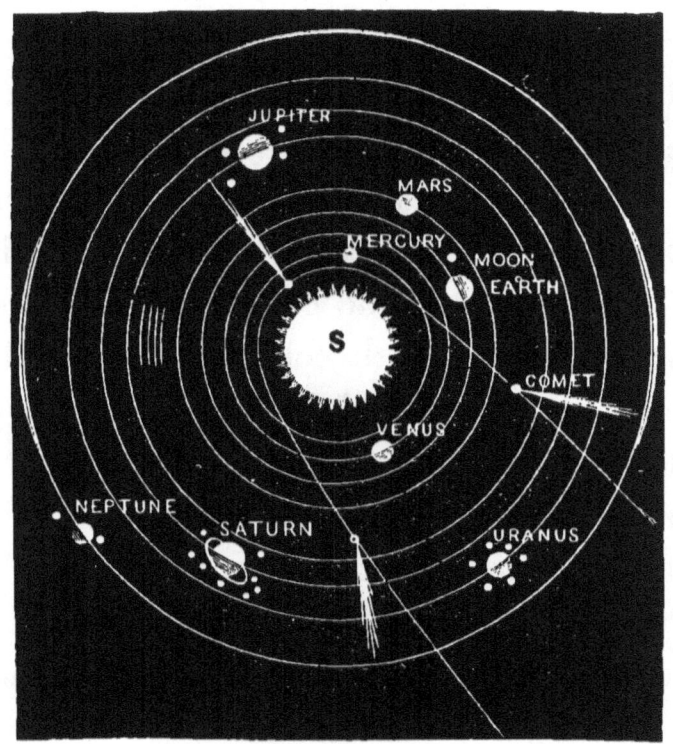

GIANT SUN AND HIS FAMILY.

estly, "but my dollie has. Nurse brought me over here, but she did not know my dollie was here. I forgot all about her yesterday, while Harry was telling me about Giant Sun, and I left

her out on the grass. But she didn't melt a bit.
I knew you wouldn't, dear little dollie, would you?
Now, dollie, sit up straight, and listen to Cousin
Mary talk. My, how she can talk, too! Can't
you?"

"I'll try," said Mary, laughing. "So you want
to hear about Giant Sun and his family. He has
such a large family, and he has to give them all
plenty of light and heat. If he put out his big
lamp in the sky, it would be always dark here, and
we would shiver with cold and die. When I
come to your room at night, Harry, to say good-
night, I always carry a lamp in my hand so that
I can see you; but supposing a puff of wind blew
it out, then I could not see you at all.

"Now this light is not only for us, but for the
rest of the sun's family as well. First, there is
little Mercury, who was named after the god of
thieves; and he deserves this name, because he
steals more light and heat from the sun than any
of the other planets."

WHAT IS A PLANET?

" What is a planet?" asked Harry.

"A planet is just like this earth we are living on, and only shines with the light it borrows from the sun. If we lived on planet Mercury, and could look at our earth, we would see it shining like a bright star in the sky; but all the light comes from the sun."

" Do we live on a star, then?" asked Nellie, her little eyes wide open with amazement.

" No; we live on a planet. We could not live on a star, as a star is blazing hot. That is the difference between a star and a planet. A star is hot and bright and shining and gives light to the planets, if it has any. Planets are little globes like the earth that circle around the sun."

" Then the sun must be a star," said Harry, " as you told me yesterday that it is very hot."

" That is right," said Mary; " and every star in the sky is a sun."

" And has lots of weensy-teensy planets going all around it?" asked Nellie excitedly.

STORY OF PLANET MERCURY.

" Some of them have, I am sure," said Mary.
" But now we are running along too fast, and
I must tell you about our own sun first, and its
nearest planet Mercury.   Well, Mercury is a very
warm little world, and it gets so near the sun that
sometimes it is about nine times as warm as here,
and at other times it is only four times as warm.
You see, Mercury does not go round the sun in a
perfect circle, so at times it is farther away than
at others.   Now, the sun is like a great fire in the
sky, and the nearer we go to it the warmer we are.
How would you like to live on a little world where
it is nine times warmer than it is here ? "

" I should not like it at all, would you, dollie ? "
said Nellie ; " we would roast if we went to world
Mercury."

" But we don't know whether there are any
people there," continued Mary, " and if there are,
they might not mind the heat at all.   You can get
used to the heat, just as Uncle Robert did when
he went to India.   Don't you remember how he

felt the change when he came home, and how he
shivered? He missed the heat just as we would

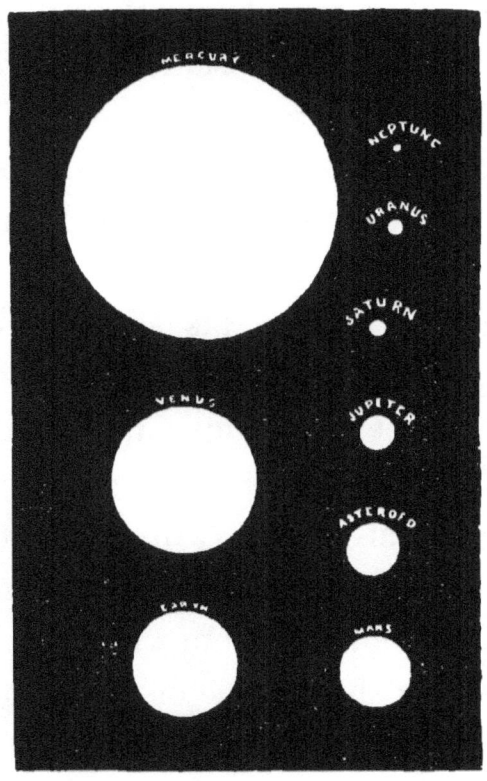

COMPARATIVE SIZE OF SUN AS SEEN FROM THE PLANETS.

suffer from it if we went to India for the first
time."

"Then Uncle Robert would not mind going to
Mercury," said Harry, laughing, "if he is getting

to like the heat in India. But I do not want him to go yet, as he might never come back again; and what would we do without him?"

"What would we?" said Nellie mournfully, her eyes filling with tears at the very thought.

"Is a planet made of earth and stones and trees and flowers, just like planet Earth?" asked Harry.

"Yes, dear," replied his sister; "only some planets, like Jupiter and Saturn, are still wrapped up in a blanket of clouds and steam, and we cannot see them yet. They are very hot indeed, and all the water that will make the oceans and seas and bays is now steam and clouds hiding the true planet from view. Water could no more rest on the surface of the planets Jupiter and Saturn than it could rest on red-hot iron. Don't you remember, the other day, when nurse upset a cup of water on the hot stove, how the water sizzled and turned into steam in a moment?

"Now planet earth, a long time ago, when it was a very young world, was very hot like Jupiter. All the lakes and seas and oceans

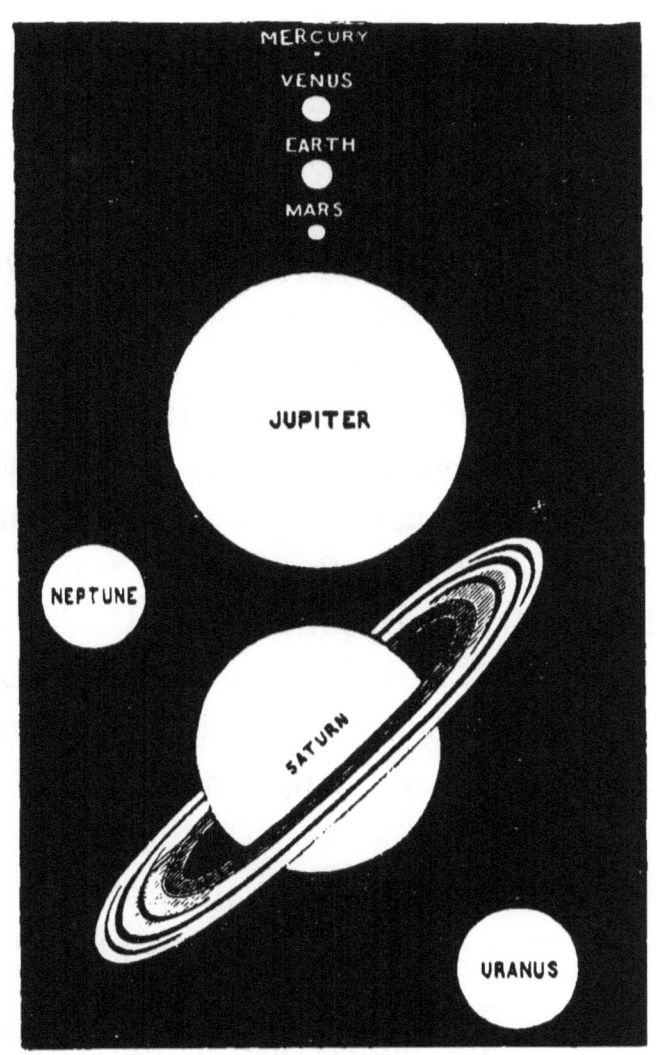

COMPARATIVE SIZE OF THE PLANETS.

were turned into steam and blankets of cloud.
It would have been a very uncomfortable world
to live on then. But it became cooler and
cooler, and the clouds changed into the oceans
and seas and lakes that make our earth so
beautiful.

"Some day this little world will grow old, and
the oceans will get smaller and smaller, and the
earth colder and colder. Then there will be
scarcely any air to breathe, and we would gasp,
and die just like that poor fish that Uncle Robert
caught last week and threw in the bottom of the
boat. Don't you remember, Nellie, how the poor
little thing gasped and jumped around? It could
not live out of the water, so it died. Now, we
cannot live without air, and if this earth had not
any air we would die. But this will not happen
for a very long time."

"Are you quite sure?" asked Harry, with an
anxious look on his face; "because I don't want
to die yet, sister."

"Quite sure, my little brother," she said, kissing him tenderly; "for hundreds and hundreds

of years must pass away before anyone will have any idea that the earth is growing old."

"And what will become of the poor little fishes when the oceans dry up?" asked Nellie sadly, as she clasped her dollie closely in her arms, as though to protect it from the coming trouble.

"I expect they will all die," said Harry wisely; "because you know, Nellie, they can't live out of water. Can they?"

"Or else that fish Uncle Robert caught would have lived," said Nellie. "But please tell us a story about Mercury, Cousin Mary, and the other little planets."

"Well, Mercury is a very little planet, and instead of taking a year of three hundred and sixty-five days, it goes around the sun in eighty-eight days. That is, it goes round the sun four times while we go round it only once. Some think Mercury always keeps the same side turned to the sun, so that it is always day on one side and night on the other, but we are not quite sure about this yet."

"I should like to live on Mercury, wouldn't

you, Harry?" said Nellie, clapping her hands
with glee. "Just think of day all the time, and
never having to go to sleep!"

"But you would get very tired of that," said
Mary, "and long for the night to come. And,
besides, would you not miss seeing the moon and
the beautiful stars?"

"I would live on the edge of Mercury," said
Harry thoughtfully, "so that when I was tired
of day I might slip around it and have night. It
must be very cold on the other side, where the
sun does not shine, if Mercury gets all its heat
from the sun."

"I suspect it is," said Mary, "and I don't
believe we should like to live on Mercury, after
all; so let us try the next planet, which is called
Venus."

STORY OF PLANET VENUS.

"What a pretty name," said Nellie; "and is
Venus very warm, like Mercury?"

"It is not so near to the sun," replied Mary,
"but it is about twice as warm and bright as our

planet. Venus is nearly as large as the earth, and sometimes she is called her twin sister.

" Like Mercury, she may probably always turn the same face to the sun, and get baked on one side and frozen on the other. She looks like a beautiful silver globe in the sky. Sometimes we see her early in the morning as a morning star, or just about twilight as an evening star. Like Mercury and the earth, she borrows all her light from the sun. We only see her because the sun is shining on her. Next to Venus is our own planet, earth, and around it circles the moon, but I must tell you about that another time."

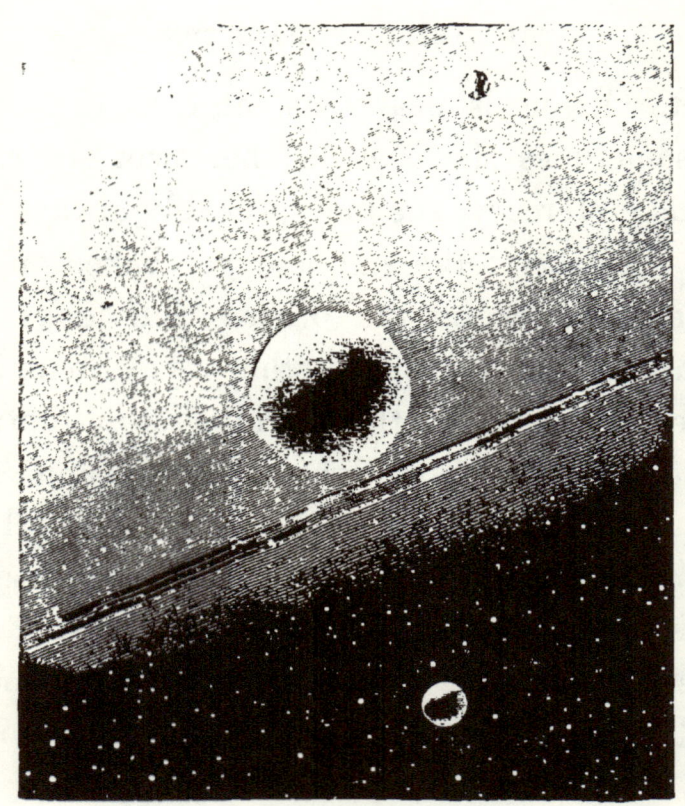

EARTH IN SPACE.

ESTELLE'S ASTRONOMY.

BY DELIA HART STONE.

Our little Estelle
   Was perplexed when she found
That this wonderful world
   That we live on is round.

How 'tis held in its place
   In its orbit so true
Was a puzzle to her,
   With no answer in view.

"It must be," said Estelle,
   "Like a ball in the air
That is hung by a string;
   But the string isn't there!"
      —*St. Nicholas*, March, 1896.

VENUS.

Fairest of stars, last in the train of night,
If better thou belong not to the dawn,
Sure pledge of day, that crown'st the smiling morn
With thy bright circlet.
      —MILTON.

THE EVENING STAR.

Lo ! in the painted oriel of the West,
  Whose panes the sunken sun incarnadines,
  Like a fair lady at her casement, shines
The evening star, the star of love and rest !
And then anon she doth herself divest
  Of all her radiant garments, and reclines
  Behind the somber screen of yonder pines,
With slumber and soft dreams of love oppressed.

O my beloved, my sweet Hesperus !
  My morning and my evening star of love !
My best and gentlest lady ! even thus,
  As that fair planet in the sky above,
Dost thou retire unto thy rest at night,
And from thy darkened window fades the light.
                              —LONGFELLOW.

MERCURY.

First, Mercury, amid full tides of light,
Rolls next the sun, through his small circle bright ;
Our earth would blaze beneath so fierce a ray,
And all its marble mountains melt away.
Fair Venus next fulfills her larger round,
With softer beams and milder glory crowned ;
Friend to mankind, she glitters from afar,
Now the bright evening, now the morning star.
                              —BAKER.

A RAMBLE ON THE MOON.

THE moon was shining brightly and flooding Harry's room with its rays. He was suffering so very much, and had tried in vain to sleep. Presently he asked his nurse if she would not let Mary come and talk to him. "It will not tire me," he begged earnestly; "and it does tire me to lie here hour after hour with no one to talk to."

His nurse understood him so well, and her heart ached for the lonely child who had so little to amuse him in life. She never refused a request if it were at all possible to grant it. So she called his sister Mary, who hastened at once to his room, and brother and sister were soon far away on a ramble in starland.

"We shall go to the moon this evening," she began, "and find out what a queer old world it is."

"Old?" asked Harry; "why do you call it

49

old, when it looks so bright and new? See, sister, how it seems to be looking right into the window and watching us. I wonder if it knows

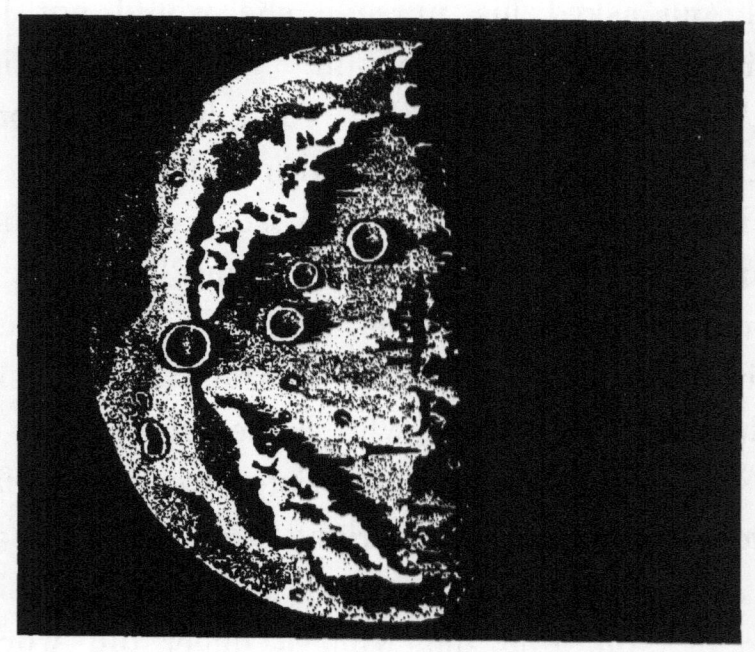

THE MOON.

what we are saying about it. Now what would it think if it heard you calling it old?"

"But it is," said Mary, laughing; "and very old indeed. Its face is wrinkled and scarred, and is just like that of the old dried-up apple we found in the orchard the other day."

"What makes it so bright, then, if it is so old?" asked Harry, as he looked curiously at the moon.

"It borrows its light from the sun," replied his sister; "if the sun were to stop shining you would not be able to see the moon at all. It would be as dark as night and twice as gloomy."

"Do you think there are people on the moon?" asked Harry excitedly.

"No, dear, not even the 'Man in the Moon,' though I am going to tell you some stories about him presently. Besides, no one could live on the moon, as there is not any air to breathe, and you cannot live without air. There is not any water to drink; in fact, there is not a drop of water on the moon."

"Then it must be very old," said Harry thoughtfully, "because you know you told me, sister, some time ago, that if a planet grows very old all the oceans and bays disappear."

"Yes, the moon is very old; it is a dead world. If you could go there, you would find it a very gloomy spot. There are no trees or flowers; and

there is not even a blade of glass. The sky is
always black and the stars shine night and day.
The shadows are so black on the moon that it
would be a fine place to play hide-and-seek. The

SCENERY ON THE MOON.

moment you stepped into a shadow you would
become invisible."

"Just like the prince in the fairy tale who put
on a little cap and no one could see him," said
Harry.

"Yes; that prince would not need the cap on
the moon. If he did not want anyone to know

he was there, all he would have to do would be to
keep in the shadow. No one would hear his foot-
steps, as not a sound can be heard on the moon.
It would be useless to speak, as there is no air to
carry the sound of a voice."

" I should not like to go to the moon, then," said
Harry seriously, " because you could not tell me
any stories, sister, could you? What would I do
then ? "

" I really cannot imagine," said Mary, laughing; " but perhaps you might come across the
Man in the Moon and talk to him in sign-
language."

" Like the deaf-and-dumb people ? " asked
Harry.

" If he could understand it," said Mary; " but
then, we know there is really not any Man in the
Moon."

" But there is a story about him," said Harry
coaxingly, " and I do wish you would tell it to
me, just now while the moon is looking at us
from the sky."

THE MAN IN THE MOON.

"Well, once upon a time," began Mary, in true fairy-story fashion, "there was a man who went out into the woods and picked up sticks on a Sunday. That was very wicked of him, you know, because Sunday is a day of rest, and picking up sticks is work. He tied the sticks together into a bundle, and, putting them on his shoulder, started to walk home with them. On the way he met a handsome stranger, who said to him :

" 'What are you picking up sticks for on Sunday ?'

" 'It does not matter to me whether it is Sunday or Monday,' replied the man roughly. 'I pick up sticks when I want to.'

" 'Very well, then,' replied the handsome stranger sternly, 'since you will not observe Sunday as a day of rest on earth, you shall have an everlasting moon-day in heaven.' Next moment he went whirling away to the sky, and landed on the moon, where you can still see him with his load of sticks on his back at full moon."

"Can I see him now, sister?" asked Harry.

"Not to-night," she replied, "because there is only a quarter moon. But perhaps you can see the face of the woman in the moon, if you look very carefully. See her sharp chin and pointed nose and shaggy eyebrows."

"Why, is there a woman in the moon, too?" asked Harry, as he looked intently at the moon, trying to see all his sister had pointed out, but having to rely largely upon his imagination.

THE WOMAN IN THE MOON.

"I have heard a story of an old woman who was sent to the moon."

"Why, what had she done?" asked Harry.

"She was very unhappy while on earth, because she could not tell when the world would come to an end; that is, when it would get old and dead like the moon, so that no one could live on it any longer. For this she was sent to the moon. She has been weaving a forehead strap ever since. Once a month she stirs a kettle of boiling hominy, and her cat sits beside her unraveling her net. So she keeps on weaving and weaving, and the cat unravels her work as soon as it is done. This must continue to the end of time, for never till then will her work be finished."

"Poor old woman!" said Harry; "I wonder she does not hide her work from the cat, or send the cat away. But then, that is only a story. Can you tell me another?"

"Do you never tire of stories?" asked Mary, smiling.

"Never, when you tell them to me, sister. And you seem to know such a lot of them."

"But these stories are only fairy-tales," said Mary, laughing; "these moon-stories, I mean."

"I don't mind," said Harry roguishly; "we must have a little make-up story now and then, or I would get tired. Do you make them all up yourself, sister?"

"No, indeed," said Mary. "I find them here and there and everywhere; sometimes right in the middle of a big book on astronomy, or in the corner of an old newspaper, or hidden away in a book covered with dust on the top shelf in the library."

"Where did you find that story about the old woman and the cat?"

"In a book of Indian legends, and the story is told by the Iroquois Indians. Here is another one I found. Would you like to hear it?"

"You know I would, dear," said Harry, nestling closer to his sister, as she clasped his hand in hers.

THE TOAD IN THE MOON.

"Once upon a time a little wolf fell very much in love with a toad, and went a-wooing one night. Just like the frog, 'he would a-wooing go.' You remember, Harry, don't you?"

"'Whether his mother would let him or no,'" continued Harry; "of course I remember all about him. So the wolf went after the toad and——"

"He prayed that the moon would light him on his way," continued Mary; "and his prayer was heard. By the clear light of the full moon he ran after the toad, and he nearly caught her, when, what do you think happened?"

"Oh, go on, sister; tell me quickly!" said Harry excitedly.

"Why, the toad jumped right onto the face of the moon, and, turning round to the wolf, said: 'How's that, Mr. Wolf?' And she is laughing at the wolf to this day."

"That was a clever little toad," said Harry, laughing; "and how vexed Mr. Wolf must have been! Are there any more people on the moon— I mean story people?"

"Yes, there is one we read about in the legend of Hiawatha. Don't you remember how Nokomis tells about a warrior

> "'. . . Who very angry
> Seized his grandmother, and threw her
> Up into the sky at midnight,
> Right against the moon he threw her:
> 'Tis her body that you see there.'"

"Do you think he meant the black marks you can see all over the moon, sister?"

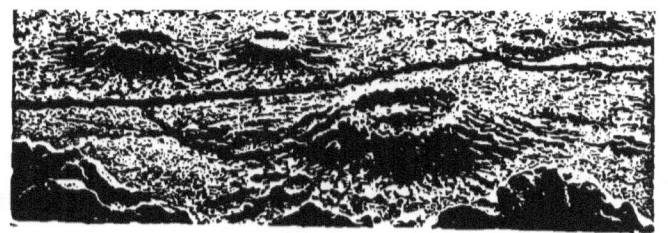

EARTH AS SEEN FROM THE MOON.

SCENERY ON THE MOON.

" Very likely," replied Mary; "and perhaps you
would like me to tell you what those black marks
are.   They are enormous plains and gloomy
caverns on the moon.   A long time ago, perhaps,
these plains were bays and seas.   At least, a great
astronomer named Galileo thought they were, and
he gave them such pretty names—the Sea of
Serenity, the Bay of Dreams, the Ocean of Storms.
But he lived in the days before it was known that
there is not any water on the surface of the moon.
Then the caverns on the moon may once have
been volcanoes pouring forth hot lava and ashes,
just as the active volcanoes on the earth.   But the
volcanoes in the moon have gone out.   They are
now like huge dark caverns, some of them more
than fifty miles across.   One is three miles deep,
and it is named Tycho, after a great astronomer of
olden times.

   " Then there are mountains on the moon just
like the mountains on earth, and quite as high.
In walking over the moon you would find it **very**

rough and uneven, but you would not mind this
very much, as you would weigh so much less.
Just think, Harry, you would weigh only one-sixth
as much as you do here."

"And what would Uncle Robert weigh ? " asked
Harry, with a gleam of mischief in his eye.

"He would only weigh forty pounds," said Mary,

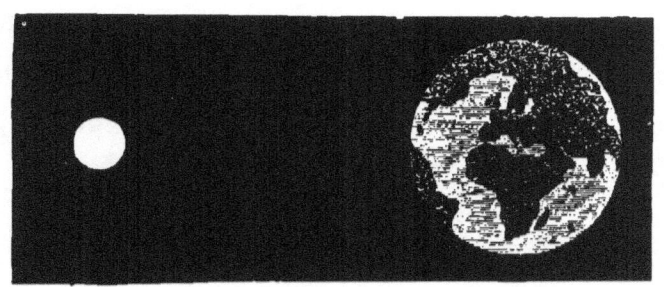

PLANET EARTH AND THE MOON.

laughing; "and if he played football on the moon,
a good kick would send the ball six times as far
away as here. Supposing we were on the moon
now, you could throw a stone at Uncle Robert's
house on the other side of the grounds, six hundred
yards away, and hit one of the windows."

"I expect Uncle Robert may be glad then we
are not on the moon," said Harry, laughing;
"because I am afraid I should be throwing stones

at the windows all the time. I can see the windows plainly from here. There is a light in the library."

"Then it must be very late," said Mary, looking over at the house; "because uncle said he would not be home till nine o'clock. So I can only tell you one more little story about the moon, and then I must let you go to sleep. This story is told by the Hindoo people, and gives the reason why the moon shines with such a soft, silvery light."

THE HINDOO LEGEND.

"The Sun, the Moon, and the Wind had been invited to dinner one day by their uncle and aunt, Thunder and Lightning. Their mother (one of the most distant stars you see far up in the sky) waited patiently at home for the return of her children. Sad to relate, the Sun and Wind were both greedy and selfish, and, while enjoying the good feast, forgot all about their poor hungry mother at home.

" But the gentle Moon did not forget, and whenever a dainty dish was placed before her she would put part of it aside for the Star who waited so patiently at home. When the Sun, Moon, and Wind returned home, the Star, who had kept her bright little eye open all night long, said:

" ' Dear children, have you brought anything home for me ? '

" Then the Sun, who was the oldest, said : ' I have brought nothing home for you. I went out to enjoy myself with my friends, not to get a dinner for my mother.'

" And the Wind said : ' Neither have I brought home anything for you, mother. You could scarcely expect me to think of you when I merely went out for my own pleasure.'

" But the gentle Moon said : ' Mother, see all the good things I saved for you,' and she placed a choice dinner before her mother.

" Then the Star turned to the Sun, and said : ' Because you went out to amuse yourself with your friends, without any thought of your poor, lonely mother at home, you shall be cursed. Henceforth your rays shall be ever hot and scorching. They shall burn all they touch, and men shall hate you and cover their heads when you appear.' That is why the sun is so hot to this day.

"Then she turned to the Wind and said: 'You also, who forgot your mother while you were enjoying yourself, shall be punished. You shall always blow during the hot, dry weather, and shall parch and shrivel all living things. Men shall detest and avoid you from this time till the end of the world.' That is why the wind is so disagreeable during the hot weather.

"But to the gentle Moon she said: 'Daughter, because you remembered your hungry mother at home, you shall be cool, calm, and bright. No dazzling glare will accompany your pure rays, and men will call you "blessed."' That is why the moon's light is so soothing and beautiful."

"Is that all?" asked Harry, as his sister finished the story.

"That is all," said Mary; "but here is a little good-night lullaby by Eugene Field, and then you must go to sleep:

" 'In through the window a moonbeam comes,
  Little gold moonbeam with misty wings,
All silently creeping, he asks, " Are you sleeping,
  Sleeping and dreaming, while the pretty stars sing ? " ' "

THE NEW MOON.

BY MRS. FOLLEN.

Dear mother, how pretty
  The moon looks to-night !
She was never so cunning before ;
  Her two little horns
  Are so sharp and bright,
I hope she'll not grow any more.

If I were up there,
  With you and my friends,
I'd rock in it nicely, you'd see ;
  I'd sit in the middle
  And hold by both ends ;
Oh, what a bright cradle 'twould be !

I would call to the stars
  To keep out of the way
Lest we should rock over their toes ;
  And then I would rock
  Till the dawn of the day,
And see where the pretty moon goes.

And there we would stay
  In the beautiful skies,
And through the bright clouds we would roam;

We would see the sun set,
And see the sun rise,
And on the next rainbow come home.
—*Taken from Child-Life, edited by* **Whittier.**

LADY MOON.

BY LORD HOUGHTON.

Lady Moon, Lady Moon, where are you roving?
    Over the sea.
Lady Moon, Lady Moon, whom are you loving?
    All that love me.

Are you not tired with rolling, and never
    Resting to sleep?
Why look so pale and so sad, as forever
    Wishing to weep?

Ask me not this, little child, if you love me;
    You are too bold;
I must obey my dear Father above me,
    And do as I'm told.

Lady Moon, Lady Moon, where are you roving?
    Over the sea.
Lady Moon, Lady Moon, whom are you loving?
    All that love me.
    —Taken from Child-Life, edited by Whittier.

A LEGEND.

A moonbeam once fell on the bell of a flower,
    Way down by a silvery rill;
'Twas cradled to sleep in a rapturous hour,
    When all the green forest was still.

That flower, when golden and glad was the morning,
    Was shriveled and wilted and thin;
But on the next night, all its chalice adorning,
    The moonbeam still lingered within.

Since then has the flower been tender and creamy,
    Wherever its petals have blown,
All fragile and pearly and dainty and dreamy
    Is the night-blooming cereus known.
    —Taken from the New York Tribune.

THE PLANET MARS AND THE BABY PLANETS.

NEXT morning Harry and his little cousin Nellie, with her doll, awaited Mary. Harry had told Nellie about his delightful ramble on the moon the evening before, and she was delighted with the stories of the man, the woman, and the toad in the moon.

"I wonder what cousin Mary will tell us about this morning," she said.

"I am going to tell you about a pretty little planet named Mars," said Mary, as she came into the room and overheard Nellie's remark. Picking up Nellie, and placing her on her knee, she began the story of Mars as follows:

STORY OF PLANET MARS.

"Next door to our own planet earth is a beautiful little world tinted with red. It has snow-white caps at the north and south poles just like

our earth, and trees and flowers perhaps far pret-
tier, for all we know. But there is not much
water on Mars, because Mars is an old planet."

"How do you know it is old?" asked Harry.

THE PLANET MARS.

"I know it is old," replied his sister, "because
the older a planet is, the smaller are the seas and
lakes and the amount of water on its surface. As
the planet gets older and older, the water dis-
appears, until not a drop is left. But there are
wonderful canals all over Mars, and if there were
boats up there, you could go all over Mars
by means of these canals. When Mr. Lowell

looked at Mars through his fine telescope, he not only saw the canals, but round spots where the canals meet."

"Perhaps the spots are landing-places where the captains take new passengers aboard," said Harry earnestly.

"Perhaps, Harry," said his sister, laughing; "that is, if there are any people on Mars, and captains and boats. How you would enjoy going in a yacht up and down these canals, seeing the lovely flowers and scenery on Mars, for I am sure it must be a very beautiful little world.

"It is not quite as bright on Mars as it is here, since it is farther away from the sun and only gets one-half as much light and heat. The year is also nearly twice as long and lasts six hundred and eighty-seven days, instead of only three hundred and sixty-five. Therefore, the summer season is nearly twice as long, but not nearly as warm as here."

"Then the winter must be twice as long and much colder than here," Harry said. "I do not think I should like that. But perhaps the canals freeze over in the winter time, and there may be fine skating up there?"

"No, the canals disappear altogether during the winter time," replied Mary; " or, rather, we cannot see them until they reappear again as faint dark

CANALS OF MARS (LOWELL).

lines in the spring-time. They get wider and wider until the summer season, then they get narrow again and disappear. Some of them are double, but the double lines we see may mean only grass and ferns on each side of a large canal fifty miles wide. When the canals double, the little round spots at the junctions of the canals darken. Perhaps these spots are like little islands in a desert, and they are covered with grass during the summer time."

"I should like to live on one of those little islands," said Harry. "Wouldn't you, Nellie?"

"If I could take my dollie with me," she replied, as she gazed at it tenderly. "And we might go for little boat-rides all around the islands. Do you think there are any little girls on Mars who have beautiful dollies like mine?"

"I really do not know," replied Mary; "but if there are any people living on Mars, I do know they are not like us. We could not live there, as there is not enough air for us to breathe. We would gasp just as that poor fish did the other day, when Uncle Robert hauled it up out of the lake and threw it into the boat. We must have air, and plenty of it, if we want to live."

"So we could not live on Mars, could we, sister?" said Harry.

"It would not be comfortable," replied Mary; "besides, it is not nearly as warm as here. Poor Uncle Robert would nearly freeze during the long winter. He would also find another surprise awaiting him if he went to Mars. Mars is a smaller world than the earth, so everything weighs less."

"Ah! I see," said Harry, clapping his hands with glee. "Uncle would not be so heavy on Mars. How glad he would be to go there! Poor Uncle Robert! He is so heavy he just shakes the house when he walks across the floor. Next time I see him I shall say : 'Go to Mars, Uncle Robert, and see what will happen to you there.' How much would he weigh on Mars?"

"He weighs two hundred and forty pounds here, and would weigh only ninety pounds there, and you would weigh only thirty pounds. So I could pick you up, couch and all, and carry you as easily as Nellie carries her doll in its doll-carriage."

"Then dollie would weigh nothing at all," said Nellie, looking at her doll curiously.

Harry looked puzzled, and after thinking a moment, he said to his sister :

"I cannot see why I would weigh less if I went to Mars."

" Because the planet being smaller than the earth, it has less power to attract you and to hold you down to its surface. The earth is like a great magnet, and if there were not something drawing us to it and keeping us there, we would be greatly puzzled. Tables and chairs would not stand firm,

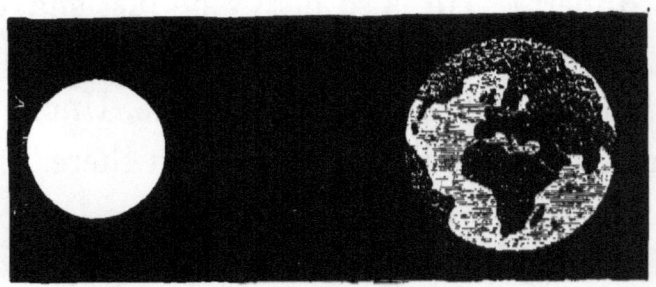

MARS AND THE EARTH.

and we would stagger about for want of weight, just as when a diver tries to walk in deep water. He has to have heavy weights fastened to him so as to keep him in place. A stone that would be quite heavy on earth would weigh only a few ounces on Mars. Nellie could carry this large rocking-chair I am sitting in and eight or ten dollies as well. Do you remember seeing the men at the circus jumping over bars five feet high? Well, on Mars they could jump fifteen feet, while the clumsy old elephant we saw there would probably be as graceful and nimble as a deer."

"How would football be on Mars?" asked Harry.

"Very unlike football here, dear. A good kick would send the ball much farther than here."

"Is Mars very far away?" asked Nellie. "If we could go there in a train, would it take us ever so long going?"

"About sixty years," said Mary, laughing, "if the train went a mile a minute. If you tried to walk it, going four miles an hour and ten hours a day, it would take you more than two thousand years to get there. So, I don't think we can take that trip, little girl, can we? But let us call on the next-door neighbor or neighbors to Mars, for there are about four hundred and fifty of them."

STORY OF THE BABY PLANETS.

"Four hundred and fifty little worlds?" asked Harry.

"Where can there be room for them all, and

don't they knock against each other in the sky ? "

" No, there is plenty of room for them up there. Besides, they are so small, some of them being only ten miles wide."

" Why, Uncle Robert walked ten miles the other day," said Harry ; " he could walk all around those little worlds. And if they are so little, I suppose he would weigh scarcely anything at all if he lived on one of them. I should think he would be almost like the giant with the seven-league boots. Don't you remember, Nellie, you were reading about him the other day. Poor little Jack the Giant Killer would not have much chance there, but perhaps he could fly if he weighed so little. And how would football be on these little worlds ? "

" You might give the ball such a kick that it would leave the planet altogether and circle around the sun as a planet on its own account."

How Harry and Nellie laughed at the idea of a football circling around the sun as a planet!

" And is this really true? " inquired Harry.

"Why, this is better than any fairy story I ever heard. Now, tell me some more. Don't you think we might be able to fly on these tiny worlds?"

"If you could get someone to make you a pair of wings up there, it would be quite easy to fly. Our bodies would only weigh a few pounds, so we ought to be able to flap a pair of wings strong enough to keep us flying. That is, if the air around these little worlds is as dense as ours."

"Don't I wish I lived there, then," said Harry regretfully, "because it would not matter about my being lame. And I could put on my wings whenever I wanted to see you, Nellie, and fly across the park, and way, way up into the sky, and——"

"Oh, don't! Harry," said Nellie, throwing her doll on the ground and catching hold of her cousin in dismay; "if you go you must take me with you too. And poor little dollie," she continued, suddenly remembering her precious charge, "and Cousin Mary and Uncle Robert and Aunt Agnes

and everybody in the world.   What would we do
if you flew away from us?"

"But I can't," said Harry, laughing at her dismay; "and it's just like a little girl to think I
would go and leave her all alone.   No, we'll all
go some day, won't we?" he continued, turning to
his sister Mary; "and we'll be with the angels—
and have wings.   You and Nellie and I—why, we
will all fly, and I shall forget I ever was lame on
planet earth then."

"And will father have wings, too?" asked Nellie
curiously.   "He will want a very big pair, something like the big eagle's down at the aquarium."

"Will he, you little rogue?" exclaimed the loud,
good-natured voice of her father, as he appeared
on the scene.   "So this is where you are, and I
have been looking for you all over the house and
grounds."

"I told nurse I would be back in a minute,"
she replied.

"A minute!" said her father, laughing heartily;
"why, you have been here nearly an hour.   So
you want your father to have wings, do you, you

little rogue! Wait till I show you how you would fly if you had wings." The next moment he put her up on his shoulder, dollie and all, and ran with her across the meadow at full speed, while she laughed merrily and clapped her hands with delight.

"So the party is broken up," said Harry's nurse, who came to look after her charge.

"Yes; one of the audience has flown," said Harry, laughing.

"And I must fly, too," said Mary, as she kissed Harry lovingly. "And I shall tell you about the rest of Giant Sun's family to-morrow. Good-by."

STORY OF JUPITER AND HIS MOONS.

It was several days before Mary could see Harry again and tell him "sky-stories," as he called them, for he had been suffering much pain. Even her gentle voice irritated him, and perfect quiet was ordered by the doctor until the little sufferer was better. At last he was able to enjoy the sunlight and the flowers and the song of the birds again, and one bright morning he was all ready, as he told his sister, to take another trip to Starland. As Mary arranged the pillows on the couch for him, and a large sunshade, so that the glare of sunlight would not hurt his eyes, he caught hold of her hand and, pressing it lovingly, he said:

"Darling, what should I do without you? You are so good to me."

"How can I help it, little sweetheart!" said Mary, as she turned her head aside to keep him from seeing the tears that would come to her eyes;

"how can I help it, when I love you so dearly. Besides, you are my own dear little brother, and you don't know how I missed you all last week."

" Did you really, sister? And I was dreaming away all day long about the wonderful stories you have been telling me. I played football on Mars, and had beautiful wings when I lived on the baby planets, and flew from one to another, and now I want to know something about the giant planets. You said they lived next door to the little tiny planets."

STORY OF JUPITER.

" Yes, next door to the baby planets we come to the largest of all, the giant planet Jupiter. If a tunnel were made through the center of Jupiter, eleven globes as large as the earth, placed side by side, would reach from one side to the other. You could make thirteen hundred globes out of planet Jupiter as large as the earth. If the earth were a large snowball, and a giant could roll thirteen hundred such snowballs into one, he would have a ball to play with as large as planet Jupiter.

If it were made of the same material as the earth, it would be more than three hundred times as heavy."

"It would take a very big giant to play with that snowball, wouldn't it?" said Harry, smiling

GIANT JUPITER AND THE EARTH.

at the thought. "There would not be much room in the sky for him to play in, would there?"

"Plenty of room," replied his sister, laughing; "room for millions and millions of balls as large as Jupiter, and much, much larger."

"What a wonderful place the sky must be!" said Harry, in awe. "Now, tell me some more

about Jupiter.   Didn't you tell me last week that
he is hidden away among blankets, and very, very
hot ? "

" That is right, Harry, but some day he will
cool down, and the blankets will change into
beautiful oceans and seas and lakes.   Then it
will be a world like ours, with trees and flowers,
and perhaps people will live there."

" The sun is so much further away from Jupiter
than from the earth that it gives it only one
twenty-seventh as much light and heat.   If you
can imagine the sun as a bright lamp in the sky,
and someone turning down the wick of the lamp
till its light is only one twenty-seventh as bright
as it is now, you can imagine how dim the light
and small the amount of heat must be on Jupiter."

" How long does Jupiter take in going round
the sun ? " asked Harry.

" About twelve years," replied Mary; " and the
day is only about ten hours long, instead of
twenty-four as here."

" What a short day ! " said Harry, in surprise
" Then you could work only five hours and sleep

five hours. I believe I would sleep all day, and all night, too. I must tell Nellie about that next time I see her."

"Why did not she come this morning, I wonder?" said Mary. "Perhaps she has gone for a walk with her nurse."

"I'll tell her about my trip," said Harry generously, "when she comes over here again. And now what else is there about Jupiter?"

JUPITER AS SEEN THROUGH A TELESCOPE.

"If you look at it through a large telescope you will see that it is beautifully colored, as if Uncle Robert had taken his paint-box, and dipped his brush into browns and reds, and tinted the cloud-belts around Jupiter here and there with touches of yellow and orange, olive-green and purple. Only an artist could get such beautiful effects. If we could journey to one of the little moons of Jupiter——"

"Has Jupiter moons also?" asked Harry, delighted at the thought.

"Five of them," said Mary; "and I shall tell you about them later. Supposing we could journey to one of these little moons, what a glorious sight Jupiter would be! From the nearest moon it would look thousands of times larger than our moon. The colors we see only faintly through our telescopes would present a magnificent sight when seen at close range, while constant changes would be taking place, as varied as the changes in the clouds flitting across a summer sky. Great cloud-masses drift hither and thither with enormous speed, driven by winds of hurricane force. By watching the changes that take place in the clouds, we know there must be winds blowing at the rate of nearly two hundred miles per hour. Do you remember the cyclone Uncle Robert told us about, when several houses were blown down and trees uprooted?"

"Yes, indeed, I do," replied Harry, "and his poor little dog Fido was nearly killed by a falling chimney."

"Poor little Fido would not have much chance on Jupiter. The storms there are ever so much worse than here.   The strongest buildings would be blown down in a few moments; sturdy oaks would be uprooted and blown about by the wind like straws."

"Do the storms last very long?" asked Harry.

"They last six and seven weeks at a time," replied Mary, "so that Jupiter would scarcely be a comfortable world to live on yet.   Besides, it is still in the fiery stage."

"Won't you tell me some more about the little moons of Jupiter?" asked Harry.

THE MOONS OF JUPITER.

"They are not so little, after all, brother, except the first one, which is only one hundred miles wide. It is such a shy little moon that it keeps hiding behind Jupiter, or gets so close to him that it is lost in the glare of light from the giant planet. We had no idea it was there at all until an American astronomer, Professor Barnard, caught sight of it one evening.   It was playing hide-and-seek as usual, but Professor Barnard, with his keen eyes, spied the little speck of light. It is now known as the fifth moon of Jupiter. It was only discovered in 1892, and just think, that for the hundreds and hundreds of years it has been there, yet no one had seen it. The French people were

JUPITER AND HIS MOONS.

so delighted because Professor Barnard caught sight of the little truant that they gave him a beautiful gold medal."

"Won't you show the little moon to me sometime?" said Harry. "I should like to see it so much."

"You can only see it through a very large telescope; but I can show you the other four moons if Uncle Robert will lend us his telescope."

"Here he comes," said Harry, in great glee, as he saw Uncle Robert crossing the meadow.

"Won't you bring over your telescope this evening?" said Harry pleadingly, as he told him what
Mary had just said.

"Certainly, my little man," his uncle replied;
"but we can only see three of the moons this
evening as one of them is eclipsed."

"What's that?" said Harry, in surprise at the
strange word.

"Eclipsed means hidden," said Mary, laughing.
"If Uncle Robert stands right in front of you, as
he is doing just now, he hides me from you, so I
am eclipsed."

"Very true," said Uncle Robert, laughing
heartily at the hint. "Planet Mary is eclipsed by
Uncle Robert, and poor little Planet Harry cannot
see her till Uncle Robert gets out of the way."
This he immediately proceeded to do, and next
moment he was pursuing Fido, who was having
a not over-friendly encounter with a strange cat
in a neighbor's garden.

"Oh, dear," said Harry, in distress, "where
were we? We were up in the sky among the
planets, and now Uncle Robert has brought us

back again to earth. Do listen to poor Fido."
He certainly seemed to be getting the worse of the
encounter with Pussy; but when Uncle Robert
came to the rescue the enemy vanished, and Fido,
nothing daunted, went in search of other prey.
When peace and quiet were once more restored,
Mary resumed her story.

ECLIPSE OF JUPITER'S MOONS.

"Do you know, the appearance and disappear-
ance of the little moons of Jupiter once gave a
great deal of trouble to astronomers. They had
a way of appearing a little too soon or a little too
late. They were very seldom on time. This was
very provoking, as astronomers were rather proud
of being able to tell exactly when these little
moons could be seen. At last they found out
what was the matter, and that they were to blame
and not the moons. We see the little moons on
account of their light, and light takes time to
travel. Don't you remember, I told you sound
travels a mile in five seconds. Light travels even

more quickly, for it only takes a little over a second in coming to us from the moon. It takes about eight minutes in coming to us from the sun; but Jupiter is about five times as far away from us as the sun, so that light takes about half an hour in coming to us from Jupiter. We do not see it as it is, but as it was more than half an hour ago, when its rays of light started out to Planet Earth.

"Now, Jupiter, in going around the sun, is sometimes on the same side of the sun as we are. Then the light from the moons reaches us in about thirty-two minutes. But when Jupiter is on the opposite side of the sun, and as far away from us as it can be, then light takes as much as forty-eight minutes in coming here—over a quarter of an hour longer. So a clever astronomer decided that when Jupiter and his moons are nearest to us, it does not take as long for their light to reach us as when they are farther away, and this is because light, like sound, must have time to travel.

"Even though light can go round the earth seven times in a second, traveling at the rate of about

186,000 miles a second, yet, as Jupiter is millions
of miles away, it takes light about half an hour,
and some times forty-eight minutes, for it to cross
that great distance. It is just the same as if
Uncle Robert were in India. It would take him a
much longer time to come and see you than if he
were at his home just a few hundred yards away.
It takes time for him to travel here, just as it
takes time for light to travel from the little
moons of Jupiter."

"I wish we had five moons shining on our
earth," said Harry; "how pretty it would be!
Does it take the moons as long as our moon to
get around Jupiter?"

"They are much livelier than our moon," replied Mary; "and the second moon flies right
around Jupiter in a little more than a day and a
half, and even the outside moon only takes about
two weeks; so there must always be a moon shining in the sky for Jupiter. These moons, except
the moon discovered by Professor Barnard, are
all larger than our moon, and the fourth one is
nearly as large as Mars. But I hear the bell for

lunch, Harry, and I must run away now. I will tell you about the other planets later."

" How many are there?" said Harry, as his sister kissed him good-by.

" Only three," replied Mary ; "and I shall tell you about them to-morrow, if you are not too tired."

"Too tired!" said Harry. "I am never too tired to listen to you."

JUPITER.

Oh ! that it were my doom to be
  The spirit of yon beauteous star,
Dwelling up there in purity,
  Alone, as all such bright things are ;
My sole employ to pray and shine,
To light my censer at the sun !
        —*Moore : Loves of the Angels.*

A LESSON IN ASTRONOMY.

The solar system puzzled us,
  Miss Mary said she thought it would,
And so she gave us each a name,
And made it all into a game,
  And then we understood.

Theresa, with her golden hair
  All loose and shining, was the sun,
And 'round her Mercury and Mars,
Venus, and all the other stars
  Stood waiting, every one.

I was the earth, with little Nell
  Beside me for the moon so round,
And Saturn had two hoops for rings,
And Mercury a pair of wings,
  And Jupiter was crowned.

Then when Miss Mary waved her hand,
  Each slow and stately in our place,
We circled round the sun until
A comet, that was little Will,
  Came rushing on through space.

He darted straight into our midst,
  He whirled among us like a flash,
The stars went flying, and the sun,
And laughing, breathless, wild with fun,
  The "system" went to smash.
                    —*Youth's Companion.*

THE GIANT PLANETS.

THE PLANET SATURN.

HARRY had spent a most delightful evening looking through Uncle Robert's telescope at the little moons of Jupiter, and he also had seen the

THE RINGED PLANET SATURN.

planet Saturn, with its rings and moons. Next evening when his sister came to talk with him he had many questions to ask her. First of all he wanted to know what the rings were made of.

"Millions of little moons," replied his sister. "I wish you could see Saturn and its rings through the great telescope at the Lick Observatory. It makes such a pretty picture? Like Jupiter, the planet Saturn is surrounded by clouds; but they are tinted with blue at the poles, yellow elsewhere, and dotted here and there with brown; purple, and red spots. Around the center is a creamy white belt. Then, there are eight moons that accompany Saturn in its journey around the sun; but they give very little light to the planet, since if they could all be full together they would give but a sixteenth part of the light we receive from the moon."

"Why is that?" asked Harry.

THE PLANET URANUS.

"Because Saturn is so far away from the Sun," replied Mary. "Next to Saturn we find Uranus. This planet was first seen by William Herschel, who afterwards became one of the greatest astronomers the world has ever known. When Herschel was a little boy his home was in Hanover. He had great talent for music, and when he was fourteen years old he joined the band of the Hanoverian Guards. What a proud boy he was when he dressed in his new uniform! However, pride must have a fall, and it was not very long before he wished he had never entered the army. Just about this time war broke out between France and England, and as Hanover belonged to the English it was attacked by the French. The Hanoverian Guards were badly defeated. Herschel spent the night after the battle hiding away in a ditch, and next day, assisted by his friends, he ran away to England. There he continued his musical studies, and some years later he became a fine organist."

"Did he have to play a big organ like the one in our church?" asked Harry.

"Something like that, I suppose," said Mary; "and he played very well indeed. He learned more and more about music, and in the evenings when going and coming from the church he used to notice the beautiful stars overhead, and he wished to learn something about them."

"Just the way I feel," said Harry. "I get nurse to pull up the window curtain at night so that I can see the stars from my bed, and they seem to laugh and wink their little eyes at me as if they knew I was watching them. Did Herschel have a telescope like the one Uncle Robert has?"

"He was not so fortunate, but he wanted one very much indeed. So he borrowed a telescope from a friend, and every night after practicing in the church he would amuse himself looking at the stars. He longed to have a telescope of his own; but he found that they cost more than he could afford to pay, so he decided to make one. He bought all that was necessary, and turned his home for the time into a workshop. He had a dear, good-natured sister named Caroline, and she did all she could to help her brother. Sometimes he was too busy to eat and she used to feed him. When he was tired she would read to him from the 'Arabian Nights.'"

"The same book I have?" asked Harry, in surprise.

"The very same; and this helped to pass away the time while Herschel polished away on the great mirror of his telescope. When the telescope was finished people came from far and near to see it. One evening when Herschel was gazing at the stars with this magic glass he spied a star not marked down on his charts. 'Something wrong here,' thought Herschel; 'this must be a comet.' But after noticing it for a while he found that it was not a comet, but a planet or wanderer among the stars."

DIFFERENCE BETWEEN A PLANET AND A STAR.

"How could he tell the difference?" asked Harry. "When I looked at Planet Jupiter last night it looked like the stars, only rounder and bigger."

"The planets are so much nearer to us than the stars that we can follow them as they slowly creep between us and the stars in their journey around the sun. The stars are so far away that we would have to watch them for thousands of years before they would seem to move at all, yet we know they are moving."

" Are the stars moving ? " said Harry, in surprise.

" Yes, they are moving, just as distant steamers seen at sea are moving ; but they are so far away that they seem motionless. Don't you remember how we used to watch them from the seashore. Still they were going as fast as steam could take them. We might compare the steamers to the stars, and the little boats nearer shore were more like the planets. We could easily follow the boats with our eyes as they danced over the waves, and in the same way we can easily follow the planets as they creep across the sky, because they are so much nearer to us than the stars."

" The new planet was called Uranus, although at first the friends of Herschel wanted to name it after him. Next to Uranus comes the planet Neptune, which was discovered before it was ever seen."

THE DISCOVERY OF PLANET NEPTUNE.

" How could that happen?" asked Harry.

" Because Uranus behaved so strangely," replied his sister. "The planets attract each other; for instance, the earth is swayed to and fro by Jupiter and Venus, and a great struggle is always going on among the planets in the family of Giant Sun. It could be plainly seen that Saturn was taking part in the struggle and dragging Uranus toward it, but something beyond the newly discovered planet was pulling it the other way. ' There must be another planet,' said the astronomers, and they were right. After puzzling over the problem two astronomers found the truant, and announced exactly when and where it was to be seen. And there it was, nearly exactly where these learned men said it would be. The new planet was christened Neptune, and it takes about one hundred and sixty-four years to go around the sun. It is so far away from the sun that it only receives one nine-hundredth of the amount of light and heat we receive on planet earth "

"Then it must be very cold on planet Neptune?" said Harry.

"And very dark also," said Mary, "since from this planet the sun only looks as large as an electric light seen at a distance of a few feet."

SIZE OF PLANETS, COMPARED WITH THE SUN.

"IS IT TRUE?"

BY MORGAN GROWTH.

She stood where the winter sunlight
　Seemed opening into the skies—
(She was only a little girl, you see,
　And her teacher was old and wise).

" You never can be promoted,"
　That wise, wise teacher said,
" For the lesson you need the most of all
　You leave unlearned, little maid."

" I didn't like to say it "—
　Her answer was grave, and slow—
" That the earth goes whirling 'round like a ball,
　For I don't see how they know.

" I'll write it down on my paper,
　(The one that I hand to you)
But when I die I shall find the Lord,
　And ask Him if it's true."

The classes were called without her,
　And the schooldays come and go,
And other children wonder and wait—
　It is hers alone to know.

Sometimes, in the empty schoolroom,
  The teacher is left alone
With the echoes that linger about the place
  And call from stone to stone.

And, lo, with this world's learning
  Before his wondering view,
He goes to his Lord—his all-wise Lord,
  And asks Him if it's true.
                    —*From Child-Study Monthly.*

COMETS AND METEORS.

A few evenings later Mary had a wonderful story to tell her brother about some visitors from space who often visit the kingdom of Giant Sun. " They are called comets, or hairy stars, but I rather enjoy calling them ' celestial tramps.' "

" What are they like ? " asked Harry.

STORY OF COMETS.

" They usually have a bright golden head, sometimes as large as the earth, and as they approach the sun they adorn themselves with a glittering train millions of miles in length. Some of the comets are regular visitors, and we know just when to expect them ; others come, and do not return for hundreds of years, while a few visit the sun never to return again."

" Where do they come from ? " asked Harry.

" We scarcely know," replied Mary, " except

that it is from outer space, just like tramps on
earth. We do not know where tramps come from,
nor do we expect to see them again. If they do
revisit us, however, we can usually recognize

A COMET.

them. Do you remember the old man who came
to the kitchen door the other day and begged for
food? You felt so sorry for him. You would know
him if you saw him again on account of his long
white beard, white hair, and shabby clothes.

"When a celestial tramp returns, however, it is

not so easy to recognize it. When it first greeted us it may have had a large head and a gorgeous train millions of miles in length. Next time we see it, how it has changed! Its head may be small, its train may have vanished, or it may be

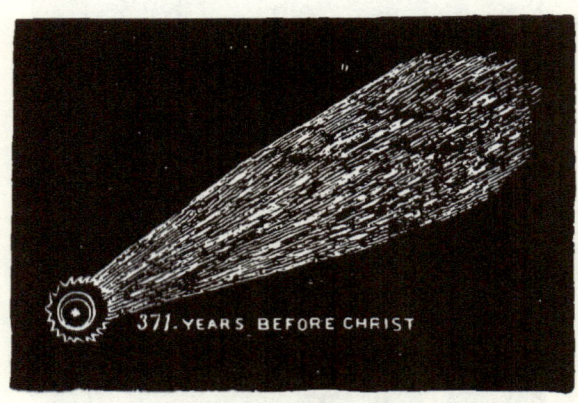

371.YEARS BEFORE CHRIST

OLD PICTURE OF A COMET.

the proud owner of three or four trains. A comet usually changes its appearance at every visit. Just as if the old man we saw the other day were to cut off his beard, dye his hair black, and wear Uncle Robert's dress-suit. We should not know him, should we, Harry?"

"I should think not," said Harry, laughing at the very idea. "Then how can you tell when the same comet visits us again?"

" Because it has a regular path marked out for it in the sky," replied Mary, " and it travels along that path unless something happens to it on the way. It may go too near giant planet Jupiter. Just like our tramp again Let us suppose he has a regular path marked out and it takes him across Uncle Robert's farm and leads to our kitchen door. We may expect to see Mr. Tramp to-morrow, but as he crosses the farm a dog bites him and frightens him away. Perhaps then we may not see him again."

" Poor old man," laughed Harry. " I hope that won't happen to him. Do the ' celestial tramps' travel very quickly through the sky ? "

" Not very quickly until they come close to the sun. Then they rush around it ever so much faster than an express train ; but as they recede from the sun they go more slowly until they seem only to creep along, as if worn out by their long journey. They also lose their trains after they go away from the sun, and the train becomes shorter and shorter, till the comet looks like a round, fluffy ball, just as it did before it came too near the sun. It is the sun's heat that drives the particles from the head of the comet and forms a train."

"What are comets made of?" asked Harry.

"Of millions of tiny little particles covered with coats of glowing gas. These particles are made up of carbon, sodium, iron, and magnesium. You will find plenty of sodium in the sea, while common table salt is partly sodium. You know what magnesium is. Some of that medicine doctor gives you is made of it."

"So if I get some iron and salt and coal and some of my medicine, and put them all together, I should have a bit of a comet," said Harry.

"But you must remember the coal, iron, sodium, and magnesium must be very much heated, and don't forget the coat of gas. Sometimes a comet breaks into pieces, and the fragments travel along by themselves as meteors."

"Sometimes the earth plunges through swarms of meteors, which journey in regular paths around the sun. At such a time, the bright masses seem to fall in showers from the sky. There are three great showers which we always know when to expect. Some come in August, some on the 13th or 14th of November, and there is another shower which always appears within a day or two of the 27th of November.

> " 'If you November's stars would see,
> From twelfth to fourteenth watching be,
> In August too stars shine from heaven,
> On nights between nine and eleven.' "

STORY OF METEORS.

" What are meteors? " asked Harry.

" Meteors are great masses of stone or iron which sometimes weigh several tons. Lieutenant Peary found one not long ago in the Arctic regions, and it weighed about eighty tons. It is lucky for us that many meteors do not fall on the earth, or we should have to walk about with iron umbrellas over our heads as a protection. When they do fall on earth, they are much prized and placed in our museums as curiosities.

" A story is told about a meteor that fell on a

farm some time ago.   The landlord said it belonged to him, for when he rented the farm to the
tenant he claimed all minerals and metals found in
the ground.

A METEOR.

" ' But it was not on the farm when the lease
was made out,' said the tenant.

" ' Then I claim it as flying game,' replied the
landlord angrily.

" ' But it has neither wings nor feathers, so I

lay claim to it as ground game,' said the tenant in reply.

" While the dispute was going on the custom-house officers seized the meteorite, because, as they said, it had come into the country without paying duty."

" That is not a true story, is it ? " asked Harry, laughing.

"Scarcely," replied Mary ; " but it was a good joke on the landlord. And now we come to the very smallest members of the family of Giant Sun. I mean the shooting stars."

" Those bright little flying stars we can see at night ? " asked Harry.

STORY OF A SHOOTING STAR.

" Yes," replied Mary ; " and if they could only talk, what a wonderful story they would have to tell ! A shooting star is very much smaller than a meteor, and the largest does not weigh more than a quarter of an ounce. You could easily hold one in your hand, for it is like a small stone, only, unlike a stone, it is always on the move. It hurries along through space ever so much faster than an express train, and all goes well as long as it keeps above the blanket of air that surrounds the earth. If it comes too near, however, it is sure to be destroyed. It dashes into the air at the rate of twenty-five miles a second, rubbing against every particle it meets on its way. This makes it intensely hot, until it glows with brilliant light. We see it for a few moments as it flashes out against the dark sky; but the light soon fades and all that remains of the shooting star is its ashes. Sometimes they sift down upon the earth and settle on the tops of high mountains, or sink into the ocean, or float in through an open window and rest upon tables and books as fine dust. But when our good housekeeper finds it there she carefully removes it with her duster. She does not know nor does she care where it came from; it certainly has no right there, and she treats it with small ceremony."

"I wonder what she would say if she knew that the dust had come from the sky," said Harry.

" I do not think it would make any difference," said Mary, laughing. "And now I am going to tell you a little story about a shooting star, and then I must say good-night.

"It is said that the evil genii—you remember reading about them in the Arabian Nights, don't you, Harry?"

"Indeed I do," he replied.

" Well, at night they are said to fly up to the gates of heaven and listen to the conversation of the angels. When the angels see their hidden foes, they hurl fiery shooting stars at them and with so good an aim that for every shooting star we may be sure there is one spirit of evil less in the world."

STARLIGHT AT SEA.

Overhead the countless stars
   Like eyes of love were beaming,
Underneath the weary Earth
   All breathless lay a-dreaming.

The twilight hours like birds flew by,
   As lightly and as free ;
Ten thousand stars were in the sky,
   Ten thousand in the sea.

For every wave with dimpled face
That leaped upon the air
Had caught a star in its embrace
And held it trembling there.
—AMELIA B. WELBY.

LICK OBSERVATORY.

STORIES OF THE SUMMER STARS.

IT was a glorious night in June, and the stars sparkled like gems against the dark background of the sky.

Harry was enjoying the scene, as the doctor had

THE GREAT BEAR.

allowed him to spend the warm summer evenings out on the lawn in front of the house. This was a royal treat to him. He could see all the sky at once, he said to his sister, and could look at the stars while she told him stories about them.   First of all, there was the Great Dipper in the North, and the Little Dipper with the Pole Star.   He was surprised when his sister said that the Great Dipper formed part of the group of stars known as the Great Bear, and he listened intently while she related the story as told in olden times by the Grecians,

LEGENDS OF THE GREAT BEAR.

"The Great Bear was said to be Calisto, the beautiful daughter of Lycaon, king of Arcadia. Juno, the wife of Jupiter, was jealous of Calisto, and threatened to destroy her beauty. Fearing that Juno would harm her, Jupiter changed her into a bear :

" ' Her arms grow shaggy and deformed with hair,
  Her nails are sharpened into pointed claws,
  Her hands bear half her weight, and turn to paws ;
  Her lips, that once could tempt a god, begin
  To grow distorted in an ugly grin ;
  And, lest the supplicating brute might reach
  The ears of Jove, she was deprived of speech.'

" Calisto had a son named Arcas, who became a great hunter. One day he roused a bear in the chase, and, not knowing that it was his mother, was about to kill her, when Jupiter, taking pity on them both, changed Arcas into the Little Bear."

" Who was Jupiter? " asked Harry.

" In the olden times, he was supposed to live on the top of Mount Olympus, with his beautiful wife Juno. When Jupiter was angry with people, it is said he would hurl thunderbolts at them, and when he was pleased he placed them after death among the stars."

" So he was pleased with Calisto and her son? " said Harry.

" So the story says," replied Mary. "But he also seemed to be afraid of his jealous wife Juno.

" A modern Greek legend gives another account of this constellation or group of stars. It is supposed that at one time the sky was made of glass and it touched the earth on both sides. It was soft and thin, and someone nailed a bear skin upon it, and the nails became stars ; and the tail is represented by the three bright stars known as the handle of the Great Dipper.

"Another story is told about a princess who was turned into a bear on account of her pride in rejecting all suitors. For this her skin was nailed to the sky as a warning to other proud maidens.

"Would you like to hear what the Indians tell about the Great Bear?" asked Mary.

"Indeed I should," replied Harry. "I had no idea the Indians looked at the stars."

"They spend so much time on the open plains that they cannot help noticing them," said Mary; "and they tell many strange legends about them. The Iroquois Indians tell the following story about the Great Bear, which must have seemed like a Bear to them, just as it did to the Grecians.

"Once upon a time a party of hunters who were in pursuit of a bear were suddenly attacked by three monster stone giants who destroyed all but three of them. These, together with the bear, were carried up to the sky by invisible hands. The bear is still being pursued by the first hunter with his bow, the second hunter carries a kettle, and the third is carrying sticks wherewith to light a fire when the bear is killed. Only in the autumn does the hunter pierce the bear with an arrow, and it is said that it is the dripping blood that tinges the autumn foliage."

"I like that story," said Harry. "Don't you know another bear story?"

"I can tell you one," replied his sister, "that is told by the Fox Indians of Louisiana. In the days of long ago the Indians believed that the trees were able to walk about at night and talk to each other. One dark night as a bear was wandering homeward through a lonely wood, he was very much surprised to see the trees walking about, nodding their heads and whispering to each other.

"At first Mr. Bear thought it was only the wind; but where he saw a mighty oak before him, the next moment it was far behind him or on the other side of the road. Presently he happened to run against a tree. It was the oak, the lord of trees. The oak was angry and reached out one of its long branches and grabbed the bear by the tail. The bear struggled all night long to get away, and at last the oak, losing all patience, gave his tail a final twist and hurled him up into the sky. They say his tail was stretched in the struggle."

STORIES OF THE GREAT DIPPER.

" That is a funny story," said Harry, enjoying the account of Mr. Bear. " Are there any stories about the Great Dipper? I wonder why it is called the 'Dipper'? "

" Because it is supposed to look like a dipper," replied Mary. " You can see the four large stars representing the dipper and the three stars that form the handle. It is known as the 'Saucepan' in the South of France, and in other parts of France it is called the 'Chariot of David.' In England it is called the 'Plow' and sometimes 'Charles's Wain.' That means wagon. In Italy it is known as the ' Car of Bootes.' Bootes was supposed to be an ox-driver and inventor of the plow—the Dipper. One day the driver, oxen, and plow were suddenly lifted off the earth and placed in the sky. You can see Bootes now, and in front of him are the seven stars of the Great

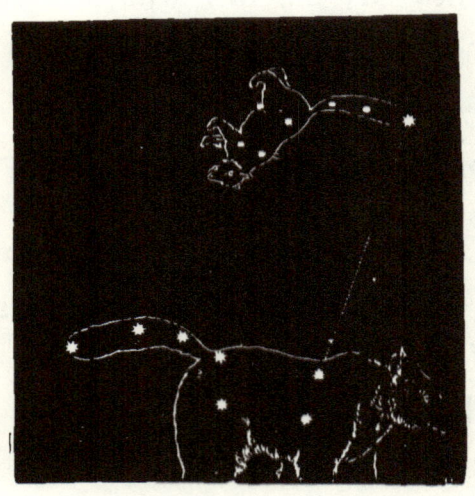

THE GREAT DIPPER AND THE LITTLE
DIPPER.

Dipper, which he must drive around the Pole Star for all eternity.

"A pretty story is told of a peasant who met our Saviour near the shores of Galilee and gave Him a ride in his wagon. As a reward he was offered a home in heaven; but he preferred to drive his wagon from east to west for all eternity, and his wish was granted. There stands his wagon in the sky, and the brightest of the three stars is called ' The Rider.'

" In North Germany ' The Rider ' is supposed to start out on his journey before midnight, and to return twenty-four hours later, his wagon turning round with a great noise. He urges on his horses with loud cries of 'hi! he!' which it is said have sometimes been heard by lucky mortals."

" Hush, sister," said Harry softly; "let us see if we can hear him now."

" No, you could only hear him at midnight," replied his sister—"that is, if the story were true."

" It is only like a fairy story, then?" asked Harry.

"All these stories are fairy stories," replied Mary; " and here is another.

" A Basque legend relates that a certain husbandman had two oxen stolen from him by two wicked thieves. He sent his laborer after them, but he did not return. Then he sent his housekeeper, and his dog, and finally he decided to go after the thieves himself. He was so angry that he lost his temper, and in punishment for the remarks he made he was condemned to continue his search through the sky for all eternity. There you can see him now. The two oxen are the first two stars, then follow the two thieves, and lastly the two servants, the husbandman, and the little dog."

" Where is the little dog?" asked Harry.

" Look at the three stars in the handle of the Dipper," replied Mary. " Now look at the middle star, and if you have good eyes you can see a little star close beside it. Here, look through this opera-glass and you can see it better."

" I see it now," said Harry, as he looked through the glasses. " So that is the little dog ? "

" Yes," replied his sister ; " and the Arabians gave it the name of Alcor."

"Dear little Alcor," said Harry, as he continued looking at him, " I am going to look for you every evening now, because I can see the Great Dipper from my window."

"So you can," replied Mary; "I forgot that it faced north.

"The American Indians tell a quaint story about the Little Dipper. Would you like to hear it?"

THE LITTLE BEAR.

"If you are not tired, sister," said Harry.

"You will get tired first, for I enjoy telling you these stories, if they amuse you, dear. Well, here is one that I came across some years ago among a collection of Indian legends.

"Once upon a time a party of Indians went out

hunting in a strange country and lost their way. They wandered about for many moons."

" What does that mean ? " asked Harry.

" I suppose they did not know anything about our months, so they counted from full moon to full moon. This shows how much they observe the sky. But, as I was saying, they wandered about for many moons, and at last the chiefs decided to hold a council and pray to the gods to show them the way home. During the dance that preceded the council, while the flames of burnt offerings were ascending to the gods, a little child appeared suddenly in their midst and said she had been sent as their guide.

" She said she was the Spirit of the Pole Star, and that if they followed where it led them they would reach their home in the far North. The hunters thanked the child, and following her advice they soon reached home. Here they held another council, and decided to call the Pole Star, ' the star which never moves,' by which name it is known among these Indians to this day.

" When the hunters died it is said they were

taken up to the sky, and we can see them still following the Pole Star. The hunters are supposed to be the stars that form the Little Dipper."

"They are smaller than the stars of the Great Dipper," said Harry, "and the dipper is smaller, but I can see it quite well. And what are the stars between the two Dippers?"

STORY OF THE DRAGON.

"They curve in and out like a great dragon," said Mary; "and two bright stars mark its eyes."

"Yes, it does look something like a dragon," said Harry. "What is its name?"

"It is called the Dragon, as that was the name given to it by the Grecians long ago. This was supposed to be the dragon that Juno placed as guardian of a tree covered with golden apples. No one dared to touch the tree while the dread monster was there. But a brave man named Hercules was not afraid, and killed the dragon. To reward it for guarding the tree Juno placed it among the stars.

" See the two bright stars that mark the eyes of the Dragon, and quite close to it is Hercules, represented in the olden maps as crushing the head of the dragon under his foot.   Bootes, who

BOOTES AND HIS HUNTING DOGS.

drives the Great Bear around the Pole Star, is very near Hercules.   There you can see him, with his hunting dogs."

" Where, sister?   I cannot see him," said Harry.

" Look right overhead, and to the west you will

see Bootes with a very bright star ; and to the east is Hercules, or the Kneeler, as he is sometimes called. Now, in between there is a pretty little half-circle of stars like a crown. This is called the Northern Crown.

STORIES OF THE NORTHERN CROWN.

"I can see that very well," replied Harry, "for it is exactly overhead, and I cannot help seeing Hercules and the Bear-driver. They are large enough," he continued, laughing. "Why are the little stars called the Northern Crown?"

"This was supposed to be a beautiful crown of seven stars given by Bacchus to Ariadne, the daughter of Minos, second king of Crete.

> " 'Her crown among the stars he placed,
>   And with an eternal constellation grac'd,
>   The golden circlet mounts, and as it flies
>   Its diamonds twinkle in the distant skies.'

"There is a pretty legend told about it by the Shawnee Indians. They call this group of stars the 'Celestial Sisters,' on account of the story, which is as follows :

" White Hawk was a great hunter, handsome,
tall, and strong. One day, while wandering
through the forest in search of game, he suddenly
found himself on the borders of a prairie. It was
covered with grass, and flowers, and a ring was
worn through the grass, without any path leading
to or from it. White Hawk was surprised at
this, so he hid behind some bushes and watched.

"'Soon he heard, high in the heavens,
    Issuing from the feathery clouds,
Sounds of music, quick descending,
    As if angels came in crowds.'

" Looking up he saw a small speck in the sky
which gradually became larger and larger. It
was a silver basket containing twelve beautiful
maidens, who leaped out as it touched the ground.
They danced around in the ring, beating time on
a silver ball. White Hawk gazed at the fairies in
wonder, and, rushing out from his hiding place,
tried to capture the youngest and prettiest. But
the sisters were too nimble for him, and, jumping into the basket, they were soon far away in
the sky.

" White Hawk was vexed, but he came again next day. This time he disguised himself as a rabbit, but one of the little sisters saw him

THE NORTHERN CROWN, AND BOOTES,
THE BEAR-DRIVER.

creeping toward them. She gave the alarm just in time for them to escape.

" Next day White Hawk disguised himself as a mouse, and hid in the stump of a tree that he had moved close to the fairy ring. The sharp-eyed little fairy noticed that the stump was not in the same place, and warned her sisters, but they only laughed at her. They even ran around it striking

it in fun. Out ran White Hawk, caught the
youngest and prettiest, and took her home as his
bride.

"For a while they were happy, but the 'Celestial Sister' became homesick, and longed for her
sisters in the sky. One day when White Hawk
was out hunting she made a silver basket and,
taking it to the fairy ring, she stepped into it,
while she sang a magic chant. White Hawk was
returning home across the fields just as the basket
rose above the tops of the trees, and, hearing the
music, he knew what had happened.

"But his wife did not forget him, and her father
sent for him and invited him to come to the sky,
where he is now one of the bright stars shining
near the Northern Crown."

"That must be the brightest star in Bootes,"
said Harry. "What is it called?"

"Arcturus," replied his sister. "Near Bootes
is Virgo, the Virgin who lived on Earth during
the Golden Age when people were very good.
Near her are the scales in which she weighed the
good and evil deeds of men.

STORY OF THE LION.

" Just above the Virgin, in the west, you can see some stars that look like a sickle," said Mary.

Harry looked in the direction pointed out by

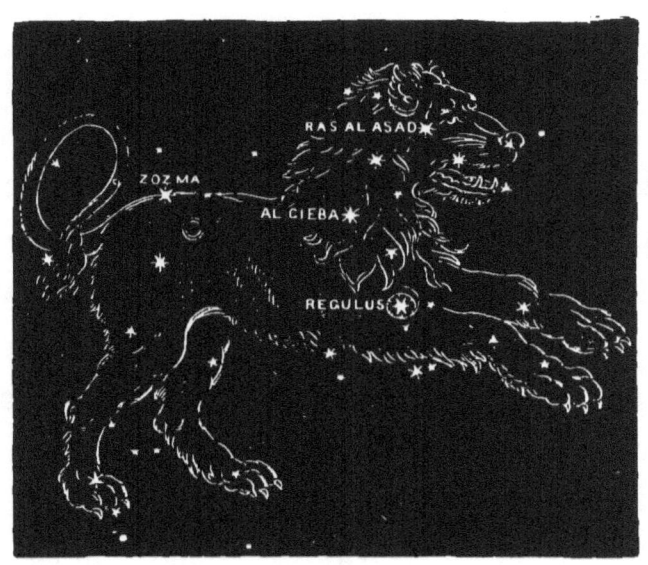

LEO, THE LION.

his sister, and there he saw the sickle plainly outlined by a few bright stars.

" Is there a story about it, sister?" he asked.

" Yes," replied his sister; " or rather there is a story not about the sickle, but about the group of stars to which it belongs, known as the constellation of the Lion.

"You remember how jealous Juno was, and she was even displeased with a brave man named Hercules, because he was afraid of nothing. She told her cousin to command Hercules to bring him the skin of a fierce lion that roamed at large through the forests. Hercules was not afraid, and attacked the lion. Finding he could not kill it with his club and arrows, he strangled the animal with his hands. He returned home carrying the dead lion on his shoulders, but Juno's cousin was so frightened at the sight of it and at this proof of the great strength of the hero that he ordered him to tell the story of his brave deeds in future at a safe distance outside the town."

"What a coward Juno's cousin must have been!" said Harry disdainfully. "I suppose Hercules laughed at him."

"Of course he did," said Mary. "But he was not the only brave man Juno disliked. Orion, the mighty hunter, also aroused her anger because he boasted that nothing could harm him. She

sent a scorpion out of the earth, and it stung him,
causing his death.   See the heart of the scorpion,

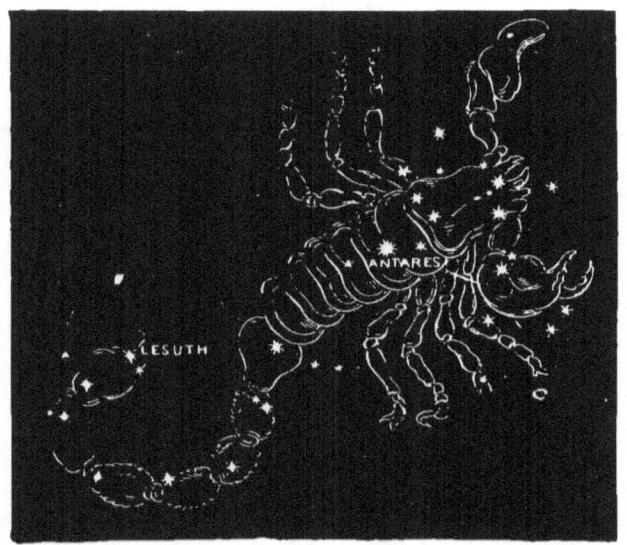

THE SCORPION.

marked by a bright red star named Antares.
Above it is the serpent and the serpent-holder.

THE MILKY WAY.

"Now look at the band of silvery light reaching
from the north to the south.   That is the Milky
Way, and it is made up of millions of bright
stars.   There are large stars and little stars, and

Professor Barnard thinks that there may be **some** very small stars forming out of the star-mist. These little stars glitter in vast beds of glowing gas. As scientists believe, this gas is the

THE MILKY WAY IS CROWDED WITH STARS.

matter from which worlds and suns are made. The stars at these points in space seem to be actually growing out of the star-mist now surrounding them. I shall show you to-morrow some fine photographs Professor Barnard **has** taken of the Milky Way where you can see this star-mist in the background of the stars.

" According to a French legend, the stars in the Milky Way are lights held by angel-spirits to show us the way to heaven. The Grecians called the Milky Way the road to the palace of heaven. On the road stand the palaces of the illustrious gods, while the common people of the skies live on either side of them.

" Even the Algonquin Indians had something to say about it, for they believed that it was the ' Path of Souls ' leading to the villages in the sun. As the spirits travel along the pathway, their blazing camp-fires may be seen as bright stars. Longfellow refers to this in his poem ' Hiawatha,' in describing the journey of Chibiabos to the land of the hereafter.

" While hunting deer he crossed the Big Sea Water and was dragged beneath the treacherous ice by evil spirits. By magic he was summoned thence, and, hearing the music and singing, he,—

" ' Came obedient to the summons,
To the doorway of the wigwam,

But to enter they forbade him.
Through a chink a coal they gave him,
Through the door a burning fire-brand.
Ruler in the Land of Spirits,
Ruler o'er the dead they made him,
Telling him a fire to kindle
For all those who died hereafter,
Camp-fires for their night encampments,
On their solitary journey
To the kingdom of Ponemah,
To the land of the hereafter.'

A SWEDISH LEGEND.

"According to a Swedish legend, there once
lived on earth two mortals who loved each other.
When they died they were doomed to dwell on
different stars, far, far apart. But, 'as they sat
and listened to the music of the spheres,' they
thought of building a bridge of light that should
reach from star to star, till it spanned the distance
separating them from each other.

"'They toiled and built a thousand years in love's all-
   powerful might,
And so the Milky Way was made a bridge of starry
   light.'

"Now, Harry, look at the Milky Way in the northern part of the sky, and what do you see?" asked Mary.

"Some stars that look like a W," replied Harry; "and just below it is another but larger W."

"The small W is Cassiopeia," said Mary, "and the large one is Cepheus; but I shall tell you their story another time, as it is getting late now. Under the large W, you will see some stars that look like a large cross. This is sometimes called the Northern Cross, but it is better known as the Swan.

LEGEND OF THE SWAN.

"The 'Swan' is supposed to represent a wonderful musician named Orpheus. Apollo gave him a magic harp, which he played with such sweetness that the wild beasts of the forest were tamed by its sounds, rapid rivers ceased to flow, and mountains and trees listened to the music.

"One day Orpheus met a beautiful maiden named Eurydice, and won her for his bride. But their happiness did not last long, as a serpent

lurking in the grass stung her foot, and she died
of the wound.

"Orpheus mourned her sadly, until at last he
died and his spirit met hers in the kingdom of

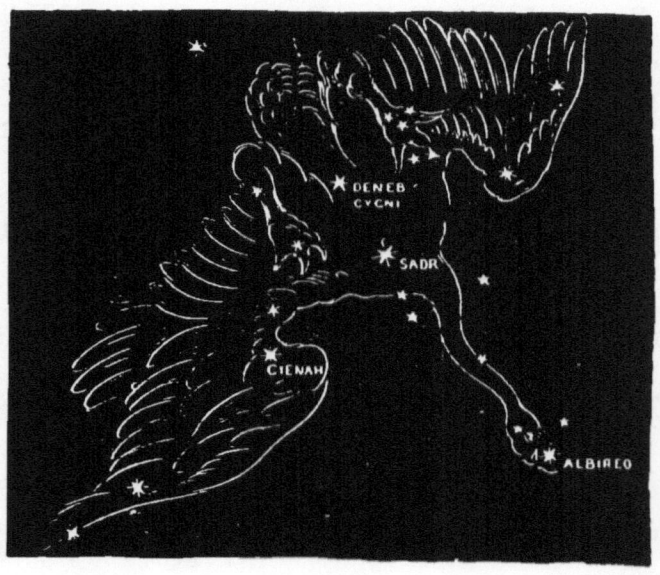

THE SWAN.

Pluto.   Afterward Orpheus and Eurydice were
placed among the stars.   You can see the harp
beside Orpheus, and it is adorned with a sparkling
blue star named Vega.

"And now one more story," said Mary, as she
heard the church clock chime nine, " and then we
must say ' good-by ' to the stars for to-night."

"It has been lovely," said Harry. "I could listen to these stories all night long. How I shall enjoy the stars since you have told me so much about them! What are you going to tell me now?"

"Just under the Swan can you see a bright star, and a little star on each side of it?" asked Mary.

Harry looked, and after a few moments he found them. When his sister had made sure that he could see the stars she meant, she began her story as follows:

MEETING OF THE STAR-LOVERS.

"The Japanese call the Milky Way the Silver River of Heaven, and they believe that on the seventh day of the seventh month (7th of July), the Shepherd-boy star and the Spinning-maiden star cross the Milky Way to meet each other. Vega, the bright star in the harp, is supposed to be the spinning-maiden, and on the other side of the Milky Way, crossing over where you see the

bright star and the little star on each side, you
will find the shepherd boy, otherwise known as
the Goat.   These stars are known among the
Japanese as the 'boy with an ox' and 'the girl
with a shuttle,' about whom the following story is
told :

"There once lived on the banks of the Silver
River of Heaven a beautiful maiden who was the
daughter of the Sun.   Night and morning she was
always weaving, blending the roseate hues of
morning with the silvery tints of evening.   That
is why she was called the Spinning maiden.   The
Sun-king chose a husband for her.   He was a
Shepherd boy who guarded his flocks on the banks
of the celestial stream.

"After   meeting   him   the   Spinning   maiden
ceased to work, and the bright hues of morning
were   left   to   take   care   of   themselves,   while   the
silvery tints of evening hung like ragged fringe on
the dark mantle of night.   The Sun-king, believing
that the Shepherd boy was to blame, banished
him to the other side of the Silver River, telling
him that only once a year, on the seventh day of

the seventh month, could the Spinning maiden
come to see him.

"The king called together myriads of doves
and commanded them to make a bridge over the
river of stars. Supported on their wings, the
Shepherd boy crossed over to the other side. No
sooner had he set foot on the opposite shore than
the doves flew away, filling the heavens with their
billing and cooing. The weeping wife and loving
husband stood awhile gazing at each other from
afar, and then they separated, one in search of
another flock of sheep, the other to ply her shuttle during the long hours of daylight.

"Thus the days passed away, and the Sun-king
rejoiced that his daughter was busy again. But
when night comes, and all the lamps of heaven are
lighted, the lovers stand beside the banks of the
starry river and gaze lovingly at each other,
eagerly awaiting the seventh day of the seventh
month. As the time draws near the Japanese are
filled with anxiety. What if it should rain, for
the River of Heaven is filled to the brim, and a
single raindrop would make it overflow! This

would cause a flood, and the bridge of doves would be swept away.

"But if the night is clear, then the Spinning maiden crosses over in safety, and meets her Shepherd boy. This she does every year except when

THE EAGLE.

it rains. That is why the Japanese hope for clear weather on the 7th of July, when the 'meeting of the star-lovers' is made a gala day all over the country."

"Sister, I can see the Spinning-maiden star, and the Shepherd boy, but where is the bridge of doves?" asked Harry.

"Across the Milky Way," said Mary.

"See the bright star, which is called Altair, and

one little star on each side. We call that the
Eagle, so if you change the story a little you can
say the Eagle takes the Spinning maiden across
the Silver River of Heaven."

THE STARS AND THE VIOLETS.

When the sky was first made and suspended
  From the far and invisible bars,
It enveloped the world, and God fashioned
  Small windows, and these are the stars.

And the bits of the sky, through the evening,
  Fluttered down to the sod and the dew,
And behold! in the morn they had blossomed,
  And these are the violets blue.

THE NIGHTS.

Oh, the Summer night
Has a smile of light
And she sits on a sapphire throne ;
  Whilst the sweet winds load her
  With garlands of odor,
From the bud to the rose o'erblown !

But the Autumn night
Has a piercing sight,
And a step both strong and free ;
  And a voice for wonder,
  Like the wrath of the thunder,
When he shouts to the stormy sea !

And the Winter night
Is all cold and white,
And she singeth a song of pain ;
Till the wild bee hummeth,
And the warm spring cometh,
When she dies in a dream of rain !
—ADELAIDE PROCTOR.

THE CALLING OF THE STARS.

God's presence through the twilight stillness glides,
   To spirits vocal—silent to the ear ;
He calls by name each fair star where it hides,
   And each star brightens, as it answers 'Here !'

Though we too call the stars, they answer not,
   They do not softly come like children shy
At a fond parent's calling, for, I wot,
   We do not know what names God calls them by.

THE GREAT TELESCOPE AT LICK OBSERVATORY.

STORIES OF THE WINTER STARS.

I heard the trailing garments of the night
    Sweep through her marble halls,
I saw her sable skirts all fringed with light
    From the celestial walls.
                   —Longfellow.

WINTER had come with its cold north winds
and frosty air. The stars glittered like gems
against the dark velvet sky, and seemed reflected
in the mantle of pure white snow that covered the
earth. Mary had asked Harry's nurse to move his
couch into her room so that he might see the stars
from the windows, one looking south, the other
east. Impatiently Harry now awaited his sister,
who had promised to take him on another trip to
starland. The room was in total darkness, and
nurse had raised the curtains. Looking right into
one window was the mighty giant Orion, while
the Twins peeped into another.

STORY OF THE ROYAL FAMILY.

"It is as good as a play," said Harry, as his sister started to tell him about them.

"First of all," she said, " I am going to tell you the story of the Royal Family, although we cannot see them from this window. You can get a glimpse of Cepheus from your own room, but the rest of the Royal Family are overhead. You would have to make a hole through the roof if you wanted to watch them while I told their story."

"If we could go out-of-doors, as we did last summer, could we see them overhead?" asked Harry.

"Yes," replied his sister; "but it is too cold now to look at them except from a warm, cozy room. To-morrow I shall show you a map of these stars, and when the days grow warm again we can look for them in the sky."

"Can you see them during the summer-time as well as the winter?" asked Harry.

"Yes, we can see them all the year round, just

as we can always see the Pole Star and the Great
Dipper. The Royal Family consists of King
Cepheus, Queen Cassiopeia, and her daughter

QUEEN CASSIOPEIA.

Andromeda, sometimes called the ' Chained Lady.'
Perseus, the rescuer, is at the feet of Andromeda,
while her head rests upon the shoulder of the
winged horse Pegasus.

"The Grecians told a wonderful story about
this family. It appears that Cassiopeia boasted
of her beauty, and said she was more attractive

than Juno, the wife of Jupiter. As for her daughter Andromeda, not a nymph in the sea could compare with her in good looks. You may im-

KING CEPHEUS.

agine how Juno and the sea-nymphs felt when they heard this vain boast!

"They determined to have revenge, and Juno asked Jupiter to punish Cassiopeia. So she was sent away from the earth and placed among the stars with her husband Cepheus.

"As for Andromeda, the sea-nymphs asked Neptune to send a sea-monster to devour her.

She was chained to a rock so that she might not escape this terrible fate; but just as the monster

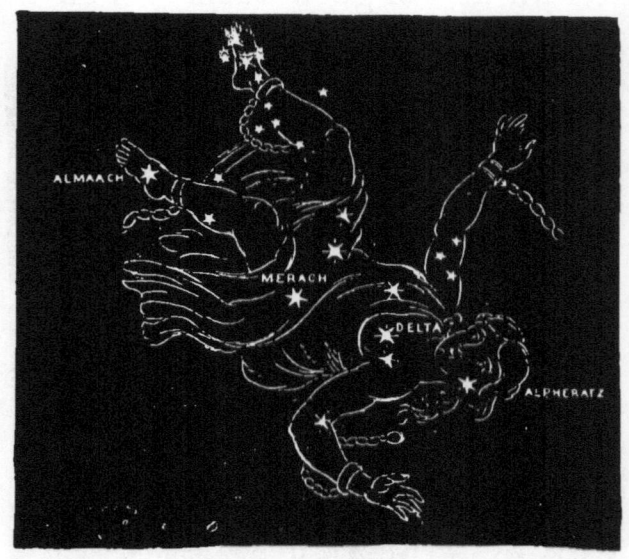

THE FAIR ANDROMEDE.

was approaching a brave hero named Perseus came to her rescue.

"Perseus was returning through the air on his winged horse Pegasus from a terrible encounter with the Gorgons. These were three sisters who frightened everyone that saw them. Serpents were wreathed around their heads instead of hair, their hands were of brass, their bodies were covered with scales, and their eyes had the power of turning all they looked at to stone. Perseus had cut off the heads of one of these terrible beings, and when he saw the monster approaching An-

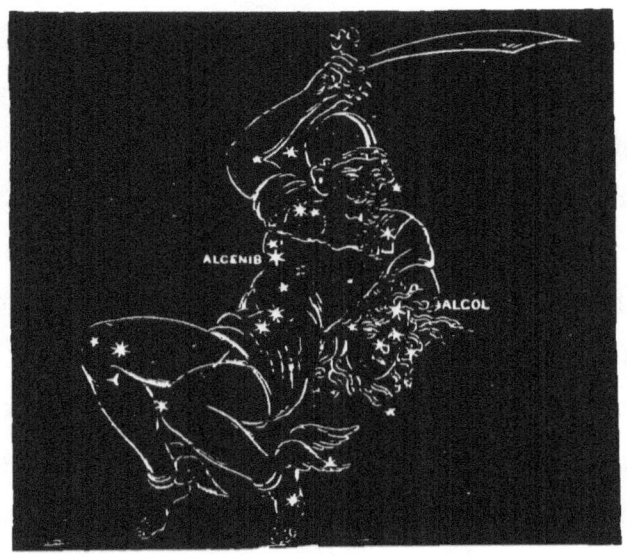

PERSEUS.

dromeda, he turned the head which he still held in his hand toward it, and in a moment it turned to stone.

"As a reward for his bravery, he was placed after his death among the stars, and near the fair Andromeda. He still holds the head in his hand,

and a star named Algol, or the Demon, as the
Arabs call it, marks the evil eye.   Sometimes it is
bright, but in a few hours it will grow dim, as
though winking at the people on earth.   For this
reason it is called a variable or changing star."

"What is that, sister?" asked Harry.

"A star that is brighter one time than another.
Supposing someone kept turning the wick of the
lamp up and down so that at one moment the
room would be very bright and the next moment
quite dim.   You would call that a changing light.
So it is with these stars, only in the case of Algol
it is a planet that goes around it and at times cuts
off part of its light.   For two days and a half it is
very bright, then during three or four hours it
begins to get dim, and remains so for twenty
minutes and then it gets bright again.

"Supposing you were trying to read by lamp-
light, and I should now and then hold a book
between the lamp and you.   Each time I did so
the light on your book would grow dim.   There
is another variable or changing star named Mira,
in the group of stars called Cetus, which is no

other than the sea-monster which was sent to devour Andromeda. You can see it if you look out of the window facing south, and you will notice that it is at a safe distance from Andromeda, who is almost exactly overhead just now.

STORY OF THE FISHES.

"Not far from the sea-monster are the Fishes, and the story about them is as follows:

"One day when Venus and her little son Cupid were walking beside the banks of a river they were frightened at seeing a terrible giant named Typhon. Flames flashed from his eyes, and as he glared at Venus and Cupid they were overcome with fear and called on Jupiter to help them. He changed them into fishes, and afterward placed them among the stars.

"Between Cetus and Orion you can see some stars winding in and out, and they are part of the River Eridanus. A daring youth named Phaeton tried to drive the chariot of the sun through the sky one day. Jupiter struck him with a thunderbolt, and hurled him from heaven into the river below.

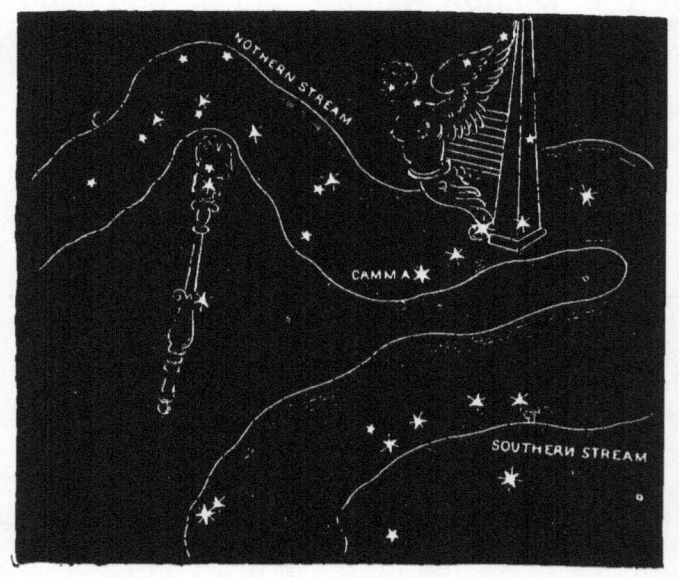

RIVER ERIDANUS.

" 'At once from life and from the chariot driven,
  Th' ambitious boy fell thunderstruck from heaven.

  .   .   .   .

  The breathless Phaeton, with flaming hair,
  Shot from the chariot like a falling star
  That in a summer's evening from the top
  Of heaven drops down, or seems at least to drop.'

" His sisters mourned his unhappy end, and were changed by Jupiter into poplars, which are

still to be seen on the banks of the River
Eridanus.

> "'All the night long their mournful watch they keep,
> And all the day stand round the tomb and weep.'"

"Poor Phaeton," said Harry, as Mary finished
the story. "And is that Phaeton with those
three bright stars near the river?"

CLOUD OF STAR-MIST IN ORION.

"No; that is Orion," replied his sister, "and
the three bright stars mark his belt. Under it
you can see a small cloud of mist, if you look
at it through your opera glass. It is clinging

around one of the faint stars in the sword. This
is star-mist, from which other stars are being
made, and it looks small only because it is so far
away from us; but there is enough star-dust
there to make thousands of bright stars. Astronomers called these clouds nebulæ."

"Who was Orion?" asked Harry. "Won't
you tell me more about him?"

"He was a mighty hunter, and in the old
maps you can see him represented as warding off
the attack of the Bull, which is glaring at him
with its bright red eye named Aldebaran. A
story was told by the Grecians about this bull:

"Once upon a time there was a beautiful little
girl named Europa, and she was a princess of
Phœnicia. One day she was playing with some
friends and gathering flowers in a meadow near
the seashore. Suddenly a snow-white bull appeared, and the little children were very much
afraid. But the princess was not afraid. She
made a pretty garland of flowers and placed it
around the bull's neck. When it knelt down in
front of her as though to thank her, she jumped

on its back, and it ran away with her down to the sea. Plunging under the waves, it swam with her to Crete. The Grecians thought they saw

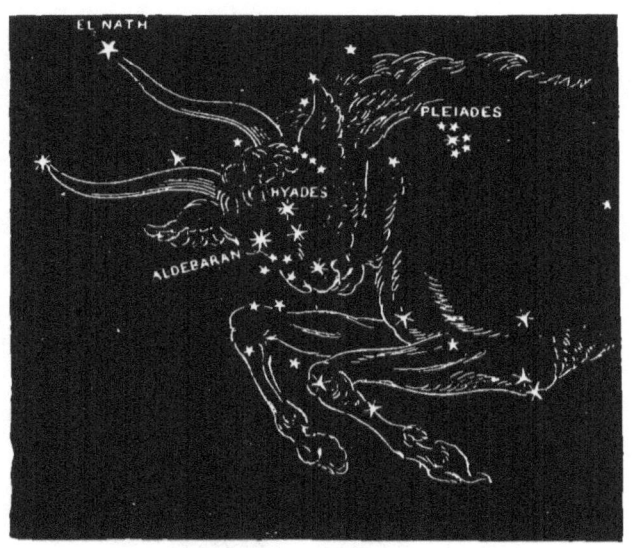

THE BULL, AND THE PLEIADES.

the bull outlined among the stars in the sky, but only its head and shoulders are there."

"But there are not any animals really in the sky, are there?" said Harry.

"No," said Mary, laughing at the question; "but if you look at the stars you can imagine you see outlines of bulls and serpents and all kinds of strange animals. Only you have to imagine very much, and this is exactly what the Grecians did.

"In the shoulder of the bull is the pretty little cluster of stars known as the Pleiades."

STORY OF THE PLEIADES.

"What is a cluster of stars?" asked Harry.

"Hundreds and thousands of stars forming

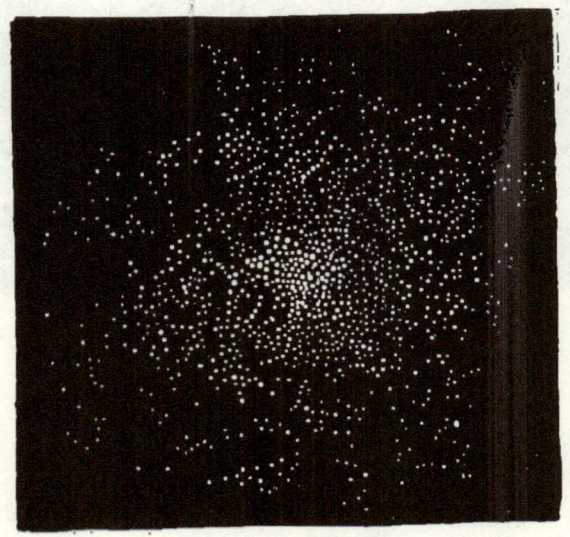

A BALL OF SUNS.

a family party, as it were; and seen from earth they seem to be closely packed together. But if we could draw near to them, however, we should find that they were very far apart. If you look at

the Pleiades through your opera glass you will
see quite a number of little stars, and if you could
see it through the large telescope at the Lick
Observatory you would be able to count hundreds
of stars. When the cluster had its photograph
taken, not long ago, six thousand stars were
counted , so you might call the Pleiades a ' ball
of suns.' There are hundreds of these clusters,
or ' family parties,' in the sky—mighty regiments
marching across the star-depths."

" What do you mean, sister ? " asked Harry in
surprise.

" All the stars are moving," replied his sister.
" Some in one direction, some in another; but
the stars in the Pleiades are all drifting in the
same direction.

" The Pleiades were said to be the seven
daughters of Atlas, and were so beautiful that
Orion pursued them across wood and dale, till the
sisters called on Jupiter to help them. He
changed them into doves, and afterward placed
them among the stars. Orion still seems to be
pursuing them among the stars ; but, strange to

say, they are drifting toward him now instead of away from him."

"Then he will soon catch them," said Harry,

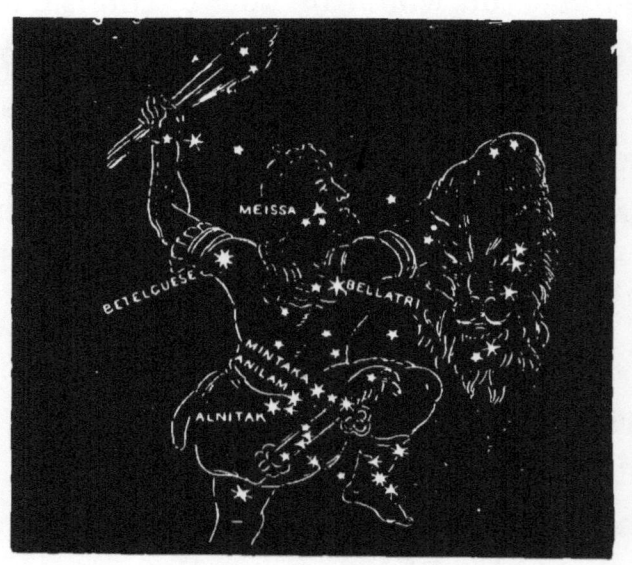

ORION, THE GREAT HUNTER.

laughing at the idea. "I once heard something about the 'Lost Pleiad.' What does that mean?"

"One of the seven stars supposed to represent the sisters does not shine as brightly as the rest, so the Grecians called it the 'Lost Pleiad.'

"Some say the Lost Pleiad is Electra, who hid her face in her hands so that she might not see the burning of Troy. But she seems to have recovered from her fright, as her star now glows as brightly as the rest. Others said it was Merope, who married a mortal while her sisters married gods.

"An Iroquois legend accounts for the Lost Pleiad by saying it is a little Indian boy in the sky who is very homesick. When he cries he covers his face with his hands and thus hides his light."

"Do tell me about him," said Harry, looking forward to a treat, as he always enjoyed these Indian stories.

"The story is as follows," said Mary:

STORY OF THE SEVEN LITTLE INDIAN BOYS.

"Once upon a time seven little Indian boys lived in a log cabin in the woods. Every evening when the stars peeped out of the sky these children would take hold of hands and dance around, while they sang the 'Song of the

Stars,' and the stars learned to love them. They would often beckon to the little boys, inviting them to come up to the sky; but the children loved their home on earth too well.

"But one day they found fault with everything. The oatmeal was too hot at breakfast, there was an absence of pie at dinner-time; and the distressing news that they were only to have corn and beans for supper was a climax to their 'tale of woe.'

"Meanwhile their mother calmly ate her supper, while her seven little boys looked on in hungry dismay. When supper-time was over they filed slowly and sadly out of the cabin. Their mother felt sorry for them, it is true; but she knew that if she gave in now she would have to give in always. She watched her boys as they danced as usual that evening and sang their song to the stars; and then she hurried into the cabin and cleared away the uneaten corn and beans.

"Alas! she did not hear the song her children sang to the stars. When the stars beckoned as usual to the little boys, inviting them to come up to the sky, they had accepted the invitation. As they danced round and round their heads and their hearts grew lighter, and in a few moments they were soaring like birds through the air. Just then their mother went to the cabin door to tell them it was time to come home; and imagine her horror when she saw her children slowly disappearing in the sky!

"And now every evening the lonely mother gazes at seven bright stars in the sky, which she fondly believes are her seven little boys, but which are really the seven stars known to us as the Pleiades. One star in the group does not shine as brightly as the rest, and this must be one of the little Indians who is homesick."

"I shall never forget that story," said Harry, who had enjoyed every word of it; "and now I wish you would tell me about that very bright star on the other side of Orion. I can only just see it, but it is so beautiful. It is bluish-white, and twinkles so brightly."

"That is Sirius, the brightest star in this part

of the sky," replied Mary, " and ever so much larger than the sun."

" What makes it twinkle ? " asked Harry.

WHY THE STARS TWINKLE.

" When we look at the stars we have to see them through the great ocean of air that surrounds the earth," replied Mary. " Like the Atlantic Ocean, when the ocean of air is disturbed there are waves, and we have to look at the stars through the waves. That is why their light seems to dance about so. When the air is still then the starlight is steady, but when it moves the stars twinkle. If we could go to the moon, where there is not any air, we would not see the stars twinkle."

" Then I should rather stay here," said Harry, " because I like to watch them dancing about. They seem so merry, I am sure they are laughing at us, sister. Is there a story about Sirius ? "

" It is part of .a group of stars named the ' Great Dog,' she replied; " and higher up you

will see the 'Little Dog.' These are the hounds
that Orion always took with him when he went

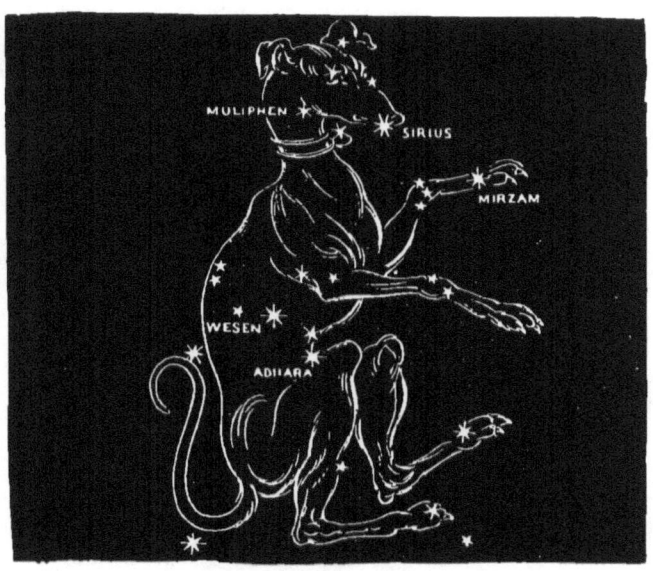

THE GREAT DOG.

hunting. They seem to have even followed him
to the sky.

"Sirius is also known as the Dog-star, because
when it was seen by the Egyptians in the east
just before dawn it was thought to announce the
overflow of the Nile. Therefore the Egyptians
watched this star, which warned them, like a
faithful dog, of the coming deluge. It was their
watch-dog or sentinel.

"Now I am going to tell you about the Twins, two brothers who loved each other dearly while on earth. They were named Castor and Pollux. Castor was killed in battle. Pollux could not

THE HEAVENLY TWINS, CASTOR AND POLLUX.

bear to remain on earth without him, so Jupiter placed him in the sky next to his brother.

"If you look through the glass you can see that Pollux is a golden-yellow star and Castor has a green tinge."

"Are all the stars colored?" asked Harry.

THE FLOWERS OF HEAVEN.

"Yes," replied his sister, "and they are as varied in color as the flowers of the earth. The stars may be called 'The flowers of heaven.' Longfellow says so beautifully :

"'Silently, one by one, in the infinite meadows of heaven
  Blossomed the lovely stars, the forget-me-nots of the
  angels.'

"Some of the natives of Australia believe that when the flowers die on earth they rise on the winds and float away to the fair fields of heaven, where they flourish forever in immortal beauty. We cannot see the colors of these flowers of heaven very well, on account of the air that sur-. rounds the earth. If it were removed, then the dark sky would seem to be covered with starry flowers of all the colors of the rainbow."

"How beautiful!" said Harry thoughtfully. "How I wish we could see them that way!"

"But even as it is," said his sister, "you can see some of these colors. Look at white Sirius, that sometimes seems to me tinged with blue, and then at red Aldebaran in the eye of the bull, and a creamy star called Capella just near the Twins. So you can see some of the colors. And now a few more words about Castor, which is a double star. That is, it is made up of two bright stars, and they go around each other.

"Professor Ball was once showing the stars through his telescope to some friends, when he pointed out this double star to them. First of all, he told them to note the different colors of the stars, for one was white, the other green. All double stars are of complementary colors. One may be green and the other red, one blue and the other orange.

"Then Professor Ball told his visitors that the stars went round each other.

"'Oh, yes!' said one of the visitors. 'I saw them going round in the telescope.'

"But it was the twinkling that made the stars appear to dance around each other. In reality, he would have had to remain with his eye at the telescope more than a hundred years before he could have seen the stars go completely around each other."

NUMBER OF THE STARS.

"I wonder how many stars there are in the sky, sister," said Harry. "Do you think we could count them?"

"I read somewhere," replied his sister, "that the stars are as plentiful as the sands on the sea-shore. Still, in the whole sky, the number bright enough to be seen without a telescope is only from six to seven thousand in a clear, moonless sky. With an opera glass you can bring the number up to one hundred thousand. A small telescope can show about three hundred thousand, while with a telescope such as the one at the Lick Observatory the number would be nearly one hundred million. But it is possible to photograph the stars, and millions of stars have had their pictures taken. Probably we would never have known anything about them but the camera caught them, and now they are being named and labeled, so that they cannot escape us again. In fact, some of the stars are so far away that if **we** had not captured them in this way they would have remained hidden to us forever."

"What do you mean, sister?" said Harry, his eyes filled with surprise.

"I mean, dear, that some stars are so far away that their light has not yet reached us. Don't you remember what I told you about Jupiter's moons: that they are so far away that light takes about half an hour in coming from them to the earth. Well, the stars are hundreds of times as far away as Jupiter's moons. So far away are they that even from the nearest—a star seen in the southern hemisphere—light takes four years and four months in reaching us, although light travels more than 186,000 miles a second.

DISTANCE OF THE STARS.

"Look at the Pole Star some night, and you will not see it as it is now, but as it was more than sixty-two years ago. All this time its light has been on its way to Planet Earth. If a planet travels around the Pole Star, or Polaris, as it is sometimes called, and an astronomer on that planet looked at the earth he would not see it as it is now, but as it was more than sixty-two years ago. There are other stars so far away that light takes hundreds of years in coming here. Perhaps they faded out long ago, but the message is still on its way. It does seem strange to think of people who may be living on distant worlds in space, watching our little world, but we need not fear. The earth is so small that it could not be seen at all, even from the nearest star. At that distance Giant Sun would not look quite as bright as Sirius does to us, and giant Planet Jupiter would only appear as a faint speck of light near the sun."

" How far away everything seems to be!" said Harry. " Yet you said just now that we could tell what the stars are made of. How can we do that ? "

WHAT ARE THE STARS MADE OF?

"The stars are made of iron, copper, zinc, and other such metals, but the heat is so intense that these metals are turned into vapor. You have seen the steam coming from the spout of a kettle when water is boiling, and you know then that the water is scalding hot. But imagine heat so great that masses of iron and copper are not only melted but turned into vapor. Then you have some idea of the intense heat that prevails on the stars. The rains that fall on earth are made up of drops of water, but the rainfalls on the stars must be drops of melting iron, while the clouds that form are sheets of molten metal."

"How wonderful!" said Harry; "and how do we know this, as the stars are so far away?"

"By means of a little instrument known as the spectroscope, or light-sifter. But you must wait till you are a little older before I can explain that to you, as it is something very difficult to understand. At any rate, I can tell you this, that when we want to find out what a star is made of

we catch a ray of its light and examine it with
the light-sifter. As Professor Ball quoted in one
of his lectures:

> " ' Twinkle, twinkle, little star,
>   Now we find out what you are,
>   When unto the midnight sky
>   We the spectroscope apply.' "

" And can you tell how old the stars are? "
asked Harry; " because when you were talking
about the planets you said some are old and some
are young."

" This same little spectroscope tells us that as
well, and we can recognize the stars that are in
their infancy, and others that are middle-aged or
nearly worn-out."

" How strange to think of worn-out stars," said
Harry; " yet I suppose they must grow old sometime, just as we do; only I suppose they take
ever so much longer growing up."

" Hundreds of years," said Mary, laughing at
the idea of grown-up stars. " There are young
stars and old stars, and even the star that gives
us light and heat will grow cold and dead some

day, and not warm its planets any longer. But that will be millions of years hence, long after we are dead and gone.

OUR ISLAND UNIVERSE.

"So it is all over the heavens. Our little universe is like an island in space. There are other islands like our own, with their millions of stars and star-clusters and star-mist, passing through the periods of youth, middle age, old age, and decay. Our little universe is not eternal. It cannot last forever, but as long as it does we should feel glad that we are here to enjoy it.

"Now, Harry, I really think we have had quite a long ramble in starland for one evening, and I believe two little stars I know need a rest."

"They are a little tired," said Harry, smiling; "two little worn-out stars, sister; and perhaps they do want to let the curtains down over them for awhile."

"I believe they do," said Mary softly; and the stars were hidden by their curtains almost before she had said the words.

WYNKEN, BLYNKEN, AND NOD.

Wynken, Blynken, and Nod, one night
  Sailed off in a wooden shoe—
Sailed on a river of crystal light
  Into a sea of dew.
" Where are you going, and what do you wish ? "
  The old man asked of the three.
" We have come to fish for the herring-fish
  That live in this beautiful sea.
  Nets of silver and gold have we,"
        Said Wynken,
          Blynken,
        And Nod.

The old Moon laughed and sang a song
  As they rocked in the wooden shoe,
And the wind that sped them all night long
  Ruffled the waves of dew.
The little stars were the herring-fish
  That lived in the beautiful sea,
" Now cast your net wherever you wish,
  Never afeared are we."
So cried the stars to the fishermen three,
        Wynken,
          Blynken,
        And Nod.

All night long their nets they threw
  For the stars in the twinkling foam;
Then down from the sky came the wooden shoe,
  Bringing those fishermen home.

'Twas all so pretty a tale, it seemed
  As if it could not be.
And some folks thought 'twas a dream they dreamed
  Of sailing that beautiful sea.
But I shall name you the fishermen three,
      Wynken,
      Blynken,
      And Nod.

Wynken and Blynken are two little eyes,
  And Nod is a little head,
And the wooden shoe that sailed the skies
  Is a wee one's trundle-bed.
So shut your eyes while mother sings
  Of wonderful sights that be;
And you shall see the beautiful things
  As you rock in the misty sea,
Where the old shoe rocked the fishermen three,
      Wynken,
      Blynken,
      And Nod.
          —EUGENE FIELD.

SEVEN LITTLE INDIAN STARS.

BY MRS. S. M. B. PIATT.

Seven little Indian boys were they,
  Dancing with the moonbeams on a mound,
In the wind they all were whirled away,
  And the fireflies searched the dews around.

Seven little Indian stars are they,
   Seven, and only one, my child, is dim.
That's the Singer, their sad stories say ;
   That's the Singer—let us pity him.

Oh, the little Singer ! (You can see
   He's not shining as the others are.)
Once, when all the stars made wishes, he
   Wished he didn't have to be a star.
              —*St. Nicholas, March*, 1890.

WHY THE STARS TWINKLE.

BY OLIVER WENDELL HOLMES.

When Eve had led her lord away,
   And Cain had killed his brother,
The stars and flowers,—the poets say,—
   Agreed with one another

To cheat the cunning tempter's art
   And show the world its duty,
By keeping on its wicked heart
   Their eyes of love and beauty.

A million sleepless lids, they say,
   Will be at least a warning ;
And so the flowers will watch by day,
   The stars from eve to morning.

On hills and prairies, fields and lawn,
   Their dewy eyes upturning,
The flowers still watch from reddening dawn
   Till western skies are burning.

Alas! each hour of daylight tells
  A tale of shame so crushing,
That some turn white as sea-bleached shells,
  And some are always blushing.

And when the patient stars look down,
  On all their light discovers,
The traitor's smile, the murderer's frown,
  The lips of lying lovers,

They try to shut their saddening eyes
  And in the vain endeavor
We see them twinkling in the skies,
  And so—they wink,—forever.
  —*Taken from The Autocrat of the Breakfast-Table.*

"GOD BLESS THE STAR!"

"Darling, I am feeling so tired this evening, won't you sit beside my bed and hold my hand in yours while you tell me about the stars?"

His sister Mary suggested lighting the lamp and reading a story, but he held her hand with gentle force, saying:

"Do not light the lamp. Leave the curtain up so that I can see the stars from my window, and tell me in your own words that story you told me of a star the other day—Dickens' story of a star. Don't you remember, sister?"

Still holding his little hand in hers, and giving it a loving pressure, she rested her head on the pillow beside his, and began, in low soft tones:

"There was once a beautiful bright star that shone down upon the home of a little boy and girl who wondered at its light. They learned to know it so well that every evening the one who saw it first would say, ' I see the star,' and before they went to sleep at night they would say ' Good-night' to the star, and, ' God bless the star ! '

" But the little girl, while she was still very young, became very weak and feeble, so that she was unable to go to the window and look at the star, so the brother would stand there alone and watch for it. As soon as he saw it he would turn round to his sister, and say, ' I see the star,' and the little sister would answer gently, ' God bless my brother and the star ! ' One evening the brother looked at the star alone, for his little sister had passed away to her home among the stars. That was a sad and lonely evening for the brother, and at night he dreamed of his sister. Her face seemed to be looking at him from the bright star, and he could see a pathway of light reaching from it to his room.

" Along the pathway were people passing from this earth to the stars. Angels waited to receive them, and as they reached the star people came out to welcome them. Kissing their friends tenderly, they went away together down avenues of light. But there was one who waited patiently near the entrance of the star and asked the guide who led the people thither if her brother had not yet come.

" ' Not yet,' he replied kindly, and as she turned sadly away the little brother reached out his arms toward her, and said, ' Here I am sister; 1 am coming to you.'

" As she turned her beaming eyes on him, the star was shining into the room, and he could see its rays of light through his tears. From that hour the child looked on that star as his future home, where he would some day meet his angel sister again.

" And he waited, oh! so patiently, and the years rolled slowly by. He grew to manhood, and still the star shone down upon him at night. Then he grew to be an old man with gray hair and wrinkled face, and his steps were slow and feeble. Others had gone before him to the star. A little brother who died while he was young—

his mother—his daughter—and now surely his own time had come.

"One night he lay upon a bed of sickness, and as his children gathered around him he suddenly cried out, as he had long ago, 'I see the star.' Then they whispered to each other, 'He is dying,' and he heard them, and said: 'I am. My age is falling from me like a mantle, and I move toward the star as a child. And, O my Father, now I thank thee that the star has so often opened to receive those dear ones who await me!'

"And next day the star was shining, and it still shines, upon his grave."

Harry had been lulled to sleep by the sound of his sister's voice, and in the dim light Mary could see that he was smiling in his dreams. Were his dreams, she wondered, about Stories of Starland?

CROSSING THE BAR.

Sunset and evening star,
  And one clear call for me !
And may there be no moaning of the bar,
  When I put off to sea.

But such a tide, as, moving, seems asleep,
  Too full for sound and foam,
When that which drew from out the boundless deep
  Turns again home.

Twilight and evening bell,
  And after that the dark !
And may there be no sadness of farewell,
  When I embark.

For tho' from out our bourne of Time and Place
  The flood may bear me far,
I hope to see my Pilot face to face
  When I have cros't the bar.
                              —TENNYSON.

YE GOLDEN LAMPS OF HEAVEN.

Ye golden lamps of heaven, farewell,
  With all your feeble light ;
Farewell, thou ever-changing Moon,
  Pale empress of the Night.

And thou, refulgent Orb of Day,
  In brighter flames arrayed ;
My soul, that springs beyond thy sphere,
  No more demands thine aid.

Ye stars are but the shining dust
  Of my divine abode,
The pavement of those heavenly courts
  Where I shall reign with God.

Father of eternal light
  Shall there his beams display,
Nor shall one moment's darkness blend
  With that unvaried day.

—PHILIP DODDRIDGE.

www.ingramcontent.com/pod-product-compliance
Lightning Source LLC
Chambersburg PA
CBHW032010060726
47497CB00017B/2905